Confessions of a Nerdy Girl:

Diary #1

TOP SECRET

by Linda Rey

www.NerdyGirlBooks.com

Confessions of a Nerdy Girl: Top Secret is a work of fiction. Names, characters, places, and incidents either are the product of the author's imagination or are used fictitiously. Any resemblance to actual persons, living or dead, events, or locales is entirely coincidental.

ISBN:978-0-9993120-2-5

Cover art by www.fiverr.com/Nizar86

Suggested ages: 10-14

Summary: *First zit … first bra … first kiss.* A twelve-year-old adopted girl shares her fears and dreams with the mother who left her at an orphanage eleven years ago.

SEE THE BOOK TRAILER HERE!
https://youtu.be/Pi4fB3yhOBE

FREE GIFT!
Thank you for purchasing
*Confessions of a Nerdy Girl: **Top Secret.***

Confessions of a Nerdy Girl

An easy peasy fill in the blank word game in Diary form.

As a thank you, I'd love to give you a FREE gift! **Nerdy Wordz** is a fill in the blank word game to play with friends — or by yourself. Create weird, wacky, and silly stories in this easy to play word game.

www.subscribepage.com/nerdywordz

See the link above.

CONTENTS

MARCH 1, 7:09 P.M.

~~Dear Diary~~,

Ugh! That looks even dumber on paper than it sounds out loud.

~~Dear Journal~~,

Nope.

~~Dear Ledger~~, Definitely not. Too CPA-ish.

Notebook? Chronicle? Log? (Log? That's ripe. What is this—Star Trek?)

Who would ever think it's this hard to begin a diary? The chances of this thing working out are pretty slim if I can't get past the first two words. And even if I figure out what to name you — you are a "you" right? Isn't that why I'm supposed to start off with a greeting ... Dear so and so, because you're like some imaginary or invisible friend? Then what? I pour out all the details of my crappy life so I can get even more depressed when I see it all in black and white? As if living through it in real time isn't bad enough?

Maybe I'm looking at this the wrong way. Maybe having a diary is supposed to be more like I'm talking to myself, a way for my conscious to communicate with my subconscious or something. If that's the case, then I guess I should start off with the words, "Dear Me."

Oh my GOSH! I am sooo overthinking this! But then I'm clinically OCD, so I overthink everything. Who CARES what I start with? It's a diary for Pete's sake, not a Master's thesis. This book even has a corny pastel cover that says WARNING! DO NOT READ! PRIVATE PROPERTY! (which of course just begs it be read by any Tom, Dick or Harry, or in my case, my sister Olivia.) It even comes with the prerequisite lock and key, which is a total joke because it's so flimsy any five-year-old with a paperclip could pick it.

My dad (he's actually my adoptive dad, but he's real to me) gave me this diary because he says he's noticed a change in me, and not for the better I'm guessing, and he thought that if I got my feelings out on paper maybe I'd get a better sense of "perspective." See things in a "different light."

He's right about the change. There'd be a change in you too if your dad came home one day and told you to start packing your stuff because the family was moving to Huntington

Beach, California, in two months.

Now, I know what you're thinking: California! The beach! Whoo hoo! Sunshine. Surfing. Bikinis. Tanned legs and blond highlights in your hair. Cute boys on skateboards, or surfboards, or boogie boards. But as they say at the Italian restaurant around the corner of my house when you ask for cheddar cheese to put on your spaghetti—fuggedaboutit.

First off, I hate the sun and it's fair to say the feeling is mutual. Ten minutes in the sun and my paper-white skin gets lobster red, until eventually it peels off in gross tissue-sized layers leaving behind, wanna guess? More white skin.

Second, I have astigmatism, so I wear thick glasses and can't see worth a darn without them, and I know for a fact the Pacific Ocean has sharks. I also know it has dolphins, but without my glasses (and maybe even with them) I'd be hard-pressed to tell the difference. A fin is a fin is a fin, especially when the saltwater is burning the crapola out of your half-blind retinas.

Third, I try NOT to go around half-naked in public because of all the hair on my arms and legs. It's black and long, and against my white skin ... Well, I'm sure you get the unattractive picture. Diane—my adoptive mom (who will never be real to me) won't let me shave my legs until next year.

She says she didn't let Olivia, her gorgeous but insanely evil daughter, shave until she was in middle school, so I can't either. I argued that in Olivia's case it didn't matter because Olivia has blond hair on her head and no visible hair anywhere on her body. Unlike me, who has to wear jeans and long sleeved shirts even during the hot humid summers in Chicago to cover up my gorilla limbs.

My argument got me nowhere if you don't count the trip to my room for an "attitude adjustment," (the seventh-grade version of time-out.) 😔

Fourth, ...

Forget fourth. Three's enough. Honestly, I could come up with about a hundred reasons why I don't want to move, but I'm running out of room on the page, plus I really have to pee.

Until next time,

Willa

P.S. Don't expect XOXO or hearts. I'm not that kind of person.

MARCH 2, 8:07 P.M.

Dear M,

There's something I really need to tell you about me. (Actually, there are a TON of things I need to tell you!)

I had a talk last night with my dad about this stupid diary, how I didn't think it would help me to sort out my feelings. Only, the thing is, when I said the word "feelings," it was like all of a sudden, I started to have them, (feelings, I mean) and I started crying like a total baby.

Eventually we got to the real cause of my recent ... I guess you could say — *depression* — regarding our move to California. He said, "Willa, are you afraid if we move you'll never have the chance of finding your birth mom?"

It's crazy, I know. Thinking that after almost twelve years you're still in the area, and someday I'd see you, maybe walking down the street or in the produce aisle of the grocery store, a woman who resembled me, only a super pretty version, and that we'd instantly know each other because of our strong genetic connection.

You would cry and apologize like crazy for leaving me and I'd forgive you. And then because you felt so bad about ditching me, I'd be able to convince you to become a home wrecker and break up my dad's marriage to Diane so he could marry you instead. The three of us would become one big happy family and live in the greater Chicago area. (Unlike Diane and Olivia, who both will have gained a hundred pounds and moved to Arkansas to marry rodeo clowns. FYI: Olivia's would have to be a shotgun wedding because Olivia's only fifteen.)

Anyway, it was my dad who suggested I should write to YOU in my diary. And not in some boring old way like "Today I got an A on my math test," but to go back in time to the beginning of my life, or as far back as I can remember, and believe me that's pretty far. Seriously. I'm not kidding. It's sort of "my thing." (I'll tell you all about it in a minute. Get ready to have your socks knocked off.) I honestly can recall with perfect accuracy, every single day of my life since the day you left me at Children's Home — which is saying something, because I was only one at the time.

My dad says someday, like, after I'm eighteen and my records are unsealed, that I might be able to find you, (if you haven't found me first) and it will make things a lot easier if I just hand you this diary with the Cliff Notes version of my life instead of unloading a bunch of rocket-fire verbal vomit on you as soon as we meet.

So I agreed with my dad that I'd write the entries in this diary to you personally. As you can see above, I'm going to start them with "Dear M," and not Dear Mom, because Diane is a total snoop, and if she found the diary she might think I was writing to her. (As if!)

I have to warn you though, my life hasn't been all rainbows and puppies.

I'm not trying to make you feel bad or

anything, but it's been pretty brutal. Especially the orphanage years before I got adopted by the Shisbey's.

I'll keep it short for now. Olivia's talons are scratching at the door, and she's screeching I used up all the hot water for my shower, so I'll write again tonight after she's asleep.

Willa

MARCH 2, 9:59 P.M.

Dear M,

I guess I'd better start off by formally introducing myself, which sounds sort of stupid considering I "sprang from your loins" as they say.

My name is Wilhelmina Eugenia Shisbey, but I go by Willa. No one ever calls me Wilhelmina Eugenia, not even my dad or Diane when I'm in trouble. It's just too many syllables or something. Anyway... my dad, Ted Shisbey, who adopted me when I was 5, said you named me "Wilhelmina" after some famous model from the 1960s, Wilhelmina Cooper, I think her name was, and not after the Ugly Betty character, Wilhelmina Slater, like I originally thought, (which would have been quite a stretch, and not because the character is black, but because she's super pretty.)

I hate to say this, M, but you sort of jinxed me setting the bar so high. Maybe if you had named me after someone, say, like, Eleanor Roosevelt, or Susan B. Anthony, inspirational women who have what my dad calls "solid faces," it wouldn't have been such a letdown. I can only imagine the thoughts that went through your mind when they handed me over and you saw my cleft lip and crossed eye, (both corrected now, in case you're wondering). I bet you felt gipped because you expected a 10 and got a 2 on the pretty baby scale.

Is that why you gave me away, I wonder?

My question is rhetorical. I'm not judging if that really is the reason. I get it. I really do. I've thrown away at least three of my favorite stuffed animals in the past year just because they lost an eye or the fur was worn in some places, so I can only imagine what it feels like to have an ugly baby. I can't say I'd do the same — give my kid away, but I'd probably want to keep them covered with a hat and a scarf until they got cuter, if I had to take them out in public.

My dad insists that is NOT why you gave me away, although he used the word "up"— not "away." (As if GAVE UP is so much better than GAVE AWAY. The result is the same.) He explained you loved me even more than most moms love their kids. That you loved me so darn much you knew I deserved a better life than the one you could give me and so that's why you brought me to the Children's

Home Society of Chicago. (He also says your loss is his gain, but I think he says it to make me feel better.)

I don't know why you really left me there after keeping me for a year, but I have two "scenarios," I guess you could call them. Do you want to hear them?

In the first scenario, my birth father — Zander, (his full name is Alexander, but he goes by Zander) finally gets that recording deal he's always dreamed of for his band and the studio insists on a world tour to promote the album. Because you sing backup for the band, (and maybe play the tambourine or something) you and Zander make the tough choice to bring me to CHSC (Children's Home Society of Chicago) with the intent on coming back to get me if the band ever folds.

FYI, they have my forwarding address.

The second scenario isn't as rosy. In that one, Zander is a Navy Seal serving his second deployment in Afghanistan, (you got pregnant when he came home on a two-week leave). But just one-month shy of my first birthday, Zander gets kidnapped by insurgents. You, desperate to find him, have to leave me at CHSC so you can join the Red Cross with the hopes of infiltrating enemy lines in order to help him escape. Only you wind up getting captured too and so now both of you are in a POW camp deep in enemy territory (with the intention of coming to get me after you're released.) So far I haven't heard about your capture in the news, but I bet there is a lot of stuff that never makes the news.

Olivia says I'm an idiot and the truth is you were probably just some "trailer park teen" who found herself in trouble, and that after one full year of looking at my ugly mug and hearing me scream all day and night you had enough of me. She says I was lucky you actually rang the doorbell and handed me off to a living person, instead of just ditching me in a dumpster behind the nearest Quick and Go. (Hopefully, someday we'll get to meet and then I'll finally know the real story.)

Now I'll tell you what I look like.

I have brown hair and brown eyes, but not like a medium brown, more like the color of Hershey's chocolate syrup. I'm not tall, but I'm not short either. I think for 12 I'm average. We don't have a scale, (Diane refuses to have one, that way she can lie and tell everyone she only weighs 115 pounds and no one can prove otherwise) but I would guess I'm about a hundred pounds. Is that fat, do you think? Olivia says it is, but that's because she's super skinny and wears size zero. (How can zero be a size? That's like saying you wear size NOTHING!) But except for some extra flab around my stomach, I wouldn't consider myself fat, exactly.

I'm not as ugly now as when you knew me, when I had that cleft lip and the one lazy eye. And if you can believe it, things got even worse for me in the looks department the first few years after you left me. For some reason, I grew too many teeth, and so I had these two extra incisors that were pointed and looked like snaggle teeth. It's not an overstatement to say I looked just like a snarling Chihuahua, between those pointed teeth and my cleft lip.

I swear, I am not dramatizing for effect. LITERALLY, the kids at the orphanage referred to me as THE SNARLING CHIHUAHUA GIRL. It wasn't just the kids who said it, either. I also heard the staff say it a couple of times, but they didn't say it to my face the way the kids did.

I'm happy to report, thanks to my dad Dr. Theodore Shisbey DDS, my cleft is gone and I have nearly perfect teeth.

That's actually how I met my dad, because of my jacked-up face and teeth. He was the dentist who used to come to the orphanage and work on our teeth pro bono — pro bono means for free. He would come every 3

months or so and bring all of his dentist stuff with him to the Home. Most of the other kids he only saw once or twice because they would get adopted pretty fast, but after 4 years, I was still there. We had this "connection," I guess you could say, maybe because we both wore glasses, but I think it had more to do with him feeling sorry no one wanted me because of how I looked.

Dr. Shisbey was the one who told the staff it would be pretty easy to fix my face, and that he'd even ask a plastic surgeon friend of his to correct the cleft (which looks like a big cut) while he pulled my extra teeth.

Since I was a little kid, I was totally freaked by the word "plastic," especially because he also used the word "Transformer." And I thought for sure that when I woke up from surgery, I would no longer be flesh and bones, but instead would be a hard plastic

Transformer, those action figure dolls that were really popular at the time.

For weeks I expected to look in the mirror and find out I had turned into molded blue plastic like Chromia, the girl Transformer. Eventually someone explained Dr. Shisbey said I would become TRANSFORMED, not become a Transformer. Truthfully, I was sort of bummed. It would have made life a lot easier to have superpowers.

I'll have to end this for now. My dad's calling through the door it's "light's out." But stay tuned, because tomorrow I'm going to tell you something really big.

Willa

MARCH 5, 6:17 P.M.

Dear M,

I know I told you I would write yesterday, but there was major drama going on around here. For once, it did not involve me, so that's good. It was Olivia, who, by the way, is now grounded for "life" according to her. (Which would only be accurate if Olivia was a housefly, because she's grounded for 2 weeks, and that's pretty much an entire lifetime for a fly.)

I won't bore you with the details about Olivia's grounding, but let's just say that when she left to go to the movies with Josh, the guy she likes, her shirt had the washing label on the inside, and when she came home, the label was on the OUTSIDE. Olivia swears she put it on inside-out from the get go, but we all know differently.

The big news I wanted to share with you is that your daughter (to be clear, I'm referring to ME; I guess I have to consider that after all this time you might have other kids) anyway, your daughter Willa is sort of famous. Not household name famous or anything, but textbook, one-of-only-a-handful-of-people-on-earth, famous.

Out of the 7.28 billion people on the planet, I'm the thirteenth person to be documented with something called H-SAM, (Highly Superior Auto-Biographical Memory). I'm right behind the actress Marilu Henner, who probably really was a household name in the olden days when she starred in the TV show "Taxi." Now she pretty much just hawks books on how to improve your memory, as far as I can tell.

So maybe you're getting all, like, Oooh ... ahhh ... Or maybe you're thinking, "I don't get what the big deal is," so I'll try to explain it.

I have an unbelievable memory.

And not just "Last Tuesday I had mac and cheese for dinner." H-SAM allows me to recall, with perfect accuracy, every single detail of every single day since the day you left me at Children's Home Society of Chicago, at one year, one day, and four hours old. (And maybe like thirty-nine minutes, but don't quote me on that.)

I don't need to write the date at the top of

each page of this diary to remind myself when I wrote it. I'm writing it down so YOU know what day it was.

For me to recall the day, I could just as easily write, "Ate Frosted Flakes. Stepped in dog poop." You of course would have no idea what that means and would probably think your kid is a total nutcase. But for me, my brain acts like the keyword search button on a computer and whether it was two years from now or ten years, I'd be able to connect the two and remember it was June 4th, (a Wednesday) four years ago. I know on that day I had Frosted Flakes for breakfast, and then I stepped in dog poop when I went out to get my dad the morning paper.

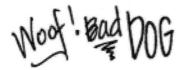

Although now that I think about it, the date could also have been August 11th, November 17th, and December 1st but not later, because Lucky, the neighbor's dog and primary poop offender, got flattened by a Fed Ex truck at noon the following day.

But if I wanted to know with 100% certainty what day it was, I could add, "Frozen Taquitos Recalled For Possible Contamination." That was the newspaper headlines of the Chicago Herald on June 4th of that year.

H-SAM doesn't mean I'm a genius or anything. In fact, I pretty much suck at math. It just means I can recall any information personally linked to me. The things I saw or heard. How things smelled or the way I felt. Really random stuff too, no matter how long ago it happened.

Monday Tuesday Wednesday Thursday Friday Saturday

For example, like, how I can remember with exact clarity Monday, March 2nd, at 10:47 a.m., the year I was in second grade, (it had rained in the morning, but the sun was shining) when Charlie Tunitski, who we called Charlie Tuna, faked us out by pretending to pull a huge green caterpillar out of his nose before eating it. Come to find out later, it was an old Gummy Worm he picked up off the floor of the lunchroom that someone had dropped next to the trashcan. I don't know how he got the whole worm jammed up his nose, but I have to say, it looked pretty realistic when he took it out.

Okay, maybe that's not a good example

because that situation was noteworthy. That's the kind of thing at our 40-year high school reunion someone will say, "Hey Charlie, remember the time in second grade when you stuffed that Gummy Worm up your nose and then ate it?"

∽ -Creepy Crawly- ∽

But what if I told you I can also remember what I was wearing that day, even though it happened almost 6 years ago? (Dora the Explorer underwear, a yellow T-shirt, elastic waist jeans, pink and yellow polka dot socks, and black sneakers.) Or what I had in my lunchbox? (PB & J on white bread, Cheetos, a juice box with apple juice, and a bruised banana — which basically made everything else taste and smell like rotten bananas.) Or that I had a scab on my elbow in the shape of Texas? Would you be impressed then?

So why haven't you heard about this girl Willa Shisbey, you might ask? Seen her on Oprah or Dr. Phil or something.

Except for the doctors at the Department of Neurology at the University of California who knew my real name, (correction: my ADOPTED name — as far as I know, you're the only one who knows my real name) I'm listed as "Subject Thirteen," or "Minor Shisbey," in all the reports and textbooks because of my age and privacy laws. (If I was over eighteen and an adult, would I have been Major Shisbey, do you think?)

Anyhow, I'm going to let you digest all this information for now and sign off until tomorrow. I'm not that tired yet, but I don't want to be a total Debbie Downer. H-SAM, come to find out, has a dark side to it. I know it probably *seems* as if remembering every day of your life would be super cool, but it just ain't so.

Until tomorrow …

Willa

P.S. FYI, I don't use the word "ain't" in everyday English. I may suck at math, but I'm an A student when it comes to English. I was using the word for EFFECT, as they say.

MARCH 8, 7:15 P.M.

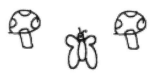

Dear M,

I don't think I'm going to be one of those people who are good at writing in their diaries every day. Some days it's all I can do to just make it through the day before collapsing into bed at night. I once said that same thing to Olivia, "It's all I can do to make it through the day," and she told me I sounded like a 70-year-old coal miner with lung disease instead of a 12-year-old nerd who'll probably die a virgin, alone, if you don't count her 6 cats. (Which is ridiculous, because I'm allergic to cats, so it would have to be my 6 dogs.)

Now I'll tell you a little more about my orphanage years. It's not exactly what most people think when you say the word "Orphanage." (But maybe you knew that already? Did you do research before taking me there?)

Anyway, when you say the word Orphanage, most people imagine some big red or gray brick building covered in soot, housing kids who speak with British accents, wear rags for clothes, and worn leather half-boot things with buttons on the sides as shoes.

In fact, our building was tan stucco, as you may recall, and we wore donated clothes, but they were halfway decent, not rags like the kids wear in orphanage movies. As far as our shoes, they were sneakers, also donated, but they were new and what the shoe factory called "Seconds," which means there was usually something wonky about them, like they were marked the wrong size or the stitching was crooked or something.

As I mentioned before, I was adopted by Ted Shisbey and his wife, Diane. In orphanage terms, I was considered an "old timer" when they adopted me because I lived at the orphanage longer than everyone else, except for a boy with cerebral palsy.

An orphanage is pretty much like a beauty pageant in that the prettiest kid wins, or in our case, gets adopted. Even biracial kids get adopted before mentally or physically handicapped ones, but then they all tend to be super cute, so there's that.

Here's an orphanage fact you won't see published in the CHSC annual report: There's always a run on black kids when a famous white person adopts one. (i.e. Madonna,

Charlize Theron, Sandra Bullock, and Angelina Jolie, just to name a few.)

Personally, I don't get it. Do people think it's cool to accessorize with a black baby? You know, to go with their Chanel sunglasses and Gucci clutch?

Not that the children weren't loved for who they are. All the kids I knew were amazing. And it wasn't as though CHSC gave the kids away willy nilly. The background checks were super extensive. I'm just calling it as I see it.

On another subject ... In case you were wondering, I think of Ted as my "DAD," and the guy who gave you his ... "seed," I guess you could say, as my "FATHER."

Diane, I DO NOT think of as anything except as my dad's wife, or Olivia's mother, even though my dad makes me call her "Mom." Most of the time, though, the word gets stuck in the back of my throat and it comes out sounding like I'm a cat coughing up a fur ball. If my dad's not around Diane prefers I call her Diane and for me to tell people she's my aunt.

As you may have guessed by now, Diane did not want to adopt me, and my dad had to talk her into it. Although Olivia says it wasn't so much of "talk" as it was "bribe," with a two-week trip to Florida.

I'm sure Florida helped, but what did it was that my dad took Diane to see the musical, "Annie." You know, the one with the curly red-headed orphan girl who can sing and dance?

I think Diane got it in her head all kids from orphanages are super talented. In her mind, we all went around singing and dancing every day. I'm sure after seeing Annie, Diane thought she'd get a singing, dancing, dishwashing little bundle of sunshine.

Instead, she got me: A scared, sullen, homely, no-talent kid with OCD and a memory like nobody's business. The only thing Diane likes about me is I can remind her of the last time she wore every outfit in her closet so she doesn't duplicate any in the same month.

Don't get me wrong, Diane isn't abusive or anything. She's never hit me, not even a spank on the butt when I was a little kid. Not that she doesn't get mad at me, she's mad plenty. I think the reason Diane has never spanked me is the same reason she's never hugged me — Diane doesn't want to touch me.

EWWW —

Sometimes I listen outside the bedroom door when my dad and Diane are talking.

Just last week Diane told my dad she can't seem to "warm up to me" yet. That she's still waiting for it to happen.

I don't think I'm overstating things when I say if it hasn't happened yet, it's never going to. Especially considering I hadn't even started kindergarten when the Shisbey's adopted me, and now I'm in middle school.

It's sort of weird, but people are always saying how much my dad and I look alike, even though we aren't genetically related. Not that my dad ever corrects people who say they notice the resemblance. Instead, he says, "We get that a lot," and then smiles and pulls me to him in a side hug.

Diane just about blows a gasket when she hears that. Her face gets all red and blotchy, and then she uses this fake voice that sounds as if she's inhaled the last bit of air from a deflating helium balloon. "Willa is actually our ADOPTED daughter," she'll explain. "Olivia is our only REAL child." Then later there's usually an argument that begins with my dad saying, "Diane, you have to stop this nonsense! How do think it makes Willa feel?"

I don't usually catch her answer because by then my head's buried underneath my bed pillows and the sound is all muffled.

Yes, my dad and I do look alike, in that we both have brown eyes, brown hair, and glasses, but I have a roundish nose (maybe like yours?) and his is definitely pointed. To see what my dad looks like — in cartoon version — pick up any Sunday Funnies and check out the *Dennis the Menace* cartoon strip. I am NOT kidding when I say my dad could have been the model for Dennis's father, Henry Mitchell. My dad looks EXACTLY like him.

When I first met my dad when he was "Dr. Ted," and years before he became my dad, he didn't have black glasses. When I first met him, they were round and wire-rimmed. He bought the black-frame plastic glasses right before he adopted me so we could be matching. He wanted me to feel better about the ugly freebie standard-issue glasses the county gave all of us orphan kids. Olivia says it lame to be twinsies with your dad, but I don't mind it.

And check this out! Now, my glasses are all the rage. Who would ever guess?!

It's some retro thing, and the look is called "Hipster," in case you're not up to date with all this teenage stuff. It's where a person with perfect 20/20 vision wears big black plastic frame glasses and sports science geek clothes that they wear in layers. But even with the same glasses and clothes there's still a huge difference between a Nerd and Hipster. From what I can tell, being a Hipster is all about attitude. Or maybe it's a money thing and a Hipster is just a Nerd whose parents are rich.

Now that you know what me and my dad look like, I'll tell you what Diane looks like. She's a vanilla-ish blond (Miss Clairol #9) and resembles those ladies on the Housewife shows. You know the ones. Those TV reality shows with the words "Real Housewife of ..." in them, with the women who show too much cleavage and wear fake eyelashes a mile long. I don't know what you think, but I seriously doubt those ladies are real housewives. I've never once seen any of them clean a toilet or make a meatloaf.

As far as Olivia's looks go, Olivia is pretty much a clone of Diane. (Only Olivia's boobs are a lot smaller and her hair is naturally blond.)

Darn! My dad is at my door saying it's way past my bedtime. (What am I? 8?) And I have to get up early tomorrow. (Which is technically correct, but I get up at the same time every school day, so there's nothing particularly special about "tomorrow.")

Anyway, bye for now.

Willa

MARCH 10, 4:59 P.M.

Dear M,

I know I haven't really told you much about H-SAM, my "special ability," as my dad calls it. We don't talk about it all that much around the house. Especially not since World War III happened, a few weeks after I was diagnosed. There was a ginormous family fight because Diane thought if I was some odd weirdo freak unusual enough to be entered into medical books and stuff, then at least the family should have the chance to make some money off it.

The short version is Diane called the local news and didn't tell my dad. They showed up in a news van about ten minutes before my dad came home from work and started in with the questions: "Willa, is it true you can remember every day of your life since you were twelve months old?" ... "Willa, as proof, can you tell us the weather temperature on June 1st, 2009?"

Which was a totally dumb question, because unless it specifically involves me in some respect, I have no idea. Did he mean what was the weather where I live? Or like in China or something?

H-SAM is sort of a me, me, me, I, I, I, affliction, in the sense I remember things that happen to me directly, but it's not like I'm Madam Cleo, the all-seeing, all-knowing, or the world weather channel. Hello!! It's called "Highly Superior AUTOBIOGRAPHICAL Memory" for a reason. (It's also called Hyperthymesia, if you want to look up more information about it.)

Now, if the news guys were SPECIFIC, and had asked me about the weather in CHICAGO on June 1st, I could have told them on that particular day, (it was a Sunday, by the way) it got as high as 63 degrees. I had to point out to the news guy I wasn't a darn thermometer, (which earned me a dirty look from Diane) and if I hadn't happened to walk by the TV when my dad was watching the news I would never have known the temperature that day (except for the general sense it was cold enough for my navy blue hoodie but not so cold I needed my pink bubble down jacket). The news guys didn't have a chance to ask much more because my dad came home from work right then and threw them all out of the house before they could ask any more questions.

I don't know how the memory recall works for the other 12 H-SAMers, but for me it works somewhat like a cross between Word Find on your computer and the Scene Selection bar in a DVD. If I connect enough words: "first day at orphanage," let's say, or a specific date, (dates are always super easy) the past basically becomes the present, and the day — as a memory — happens all over again in the NOW, if that makes sense. (Think of it as traveling back in time only you never actually leave.)

If I wanted to recall a specific birthday of mine I could scroll through ... I guess I could call them thumbnail pictures in my mind, and then select whichever one I needed to recall. It then opens up the full scene, and I'm back in that moment — feeling every thought and emotion with the same intensity as I did the first time.

Seems pretty cool, right?

Only, it's not cool. Not at all. In fact, it's a curse. An awful, terrible, no good, rotten curse.

Unlike normal people, I'm constantly jumping from past to present in my head, and so half of the time I'm stuck in a haze of H-SAM purgatory where I'm trying to stay in the present and not let some image or word pull me back to any number of the horrendous days of my life with the same gut-punching intensity.

Like right now, I'm remembering the second Sunday in August when I was 4, and Mr. and Mrs. Hernandez, who were shopping for a girl between the age of 3 and 7, said "No. Not that girl," when I was offered as a choice, "We'll take the cute one instead, the girl with the blond hair," referring to Julie, two girls down in the lineup.

It wasn't a total surprise they chose Julie, because the other choices were Bonnie, who was covered in chicken pox scabs at the time, or Lucy, whose head was shaved bald as a baby's behind as a remedy for a pesky lice issue she'd been dealing with. Still, it hurt my feelings not to be chosen again, and I blubbered like a baby when the staff told me I was dismissed and could go back to my room.

And I know it will make me sound like a total

wuss, but right now my eyes are tearing up and I'm feeling like my four-year-old self again and have an insane urge to suck my thumb. Not that I'd do it, but still, the urge is pretty strong.

Geeze! Now I've opened the floodgates to the "line-up" memories and the last Saturday in May the year I was three has popped in my head. That was the day I got presented to Mr. Simon and Mr. Peters, who I now know where a gay couple, but who at the time I thought were brothers who looked nothing alike. It was Mr. Peters who said in a snippy tone, "No, we'd prefer our child's eyes NOT be crossed."

At three I didn't get the concept of irony, but it just so happens Mr. Simon had a crab eye almost as bad as mine, so I can only assume what they say is true: Love is blind. (Unless of course Mr. Peters' reasoning was that one cross-eyed person in the family was enough.)

I could give more examples, but my dad's warned me not to go into too much detail about all the bad stuff. He says it might make you sad or seem as if I'm trying to blame you or something. Plus, he said the past can't be changed, so there's no sense in dwelling on it. An easy thing for him to say, because for H-SAMers, dwelling is our specialty.

Memories Remember WHEN ?...

Over the years I've played the "Would I Rather ..." game when it comes to H-SAM. It's a game where you have two equally bad options but you must still choose one of them. Like, "If I had a choice, would I rather have cystic acne — or chronic bad breath?" ... "Would I rather be the tallest kid in my school — or the shortest?" "Would I rather have freckles covering my entire body — or a hooked nose?" Etc.

So far I'm willing to give up toes or fingers in exchange for NOT having H-SAM, or maybe a couple of each, but not give up my eyesight or a major limb. I'd also trade never going to prom (which Olivia says is stupid, because I'm never going to get asked to prom, period, so the point is "moot.")

I'm going to end this now because my brain is starting to swell with negativity and I need a reset. (Don't be alarmed, it's nothing that requires a doctor or anything.) A reset means I make myself a chocolate sundae. It's something my dad came up with when my mind gets stuck in the past. Making the sundae puts me in task mode, according to my dad, and then eating the chocolate floods my brain with endorphins that bind with the opiate receptors and lead to feelings of euphoria and wellbeing ... or something like that.

Hasta la vista!

Willa

P.S. Hasta la vista is Spanish for "See you later," in case you were wondering.

MARCH 11, 6:31 P.M.

Dear M,

Have you ever read the book "Are You There God? It's Me, Margaret."?? (And I'm intentionally putting the question marks on the outside of the quotes or it will look as if Margaret isn't quite sure what her name is.)

The book was written in the 70s, so maybe it was even before your era, but it's considered a Classic. It's about a girl who, now that I think about it, probably had OCD like me, because she is constantly obsessing over the dumbest things. One of the things is her period. Or lack of it, I guess I should say. Margaret and her friends CAN NOT WAIT to get their periods! Which, if they had an older sister, they would know how dumb it is to want to get something that involves large amounts of blood pouring from strange openings in your body and having to either stuff things up that opening or wear thick padding between your legs to absorb it.

Ewww ...

The whole thing sounds pretty gross to me, and I am in no hurry, WHATSOEVER, to get mine. The only reason I'm even bringing it up is because I learned mothers and daughters sometimes start theirs at the same age, and so I thought it might be nice to have a heads-up, so I could be prepared. Like, should I be checking my underwear every day now that I'm 12? Or should I just relax and start stressing about it next year instead?

My dad told me to ask Diane about it, but

there is NO WAY I'm asking her. Especially not after the bra fiasco.

Here's what happened ... It's not like I really needed a REAL bra (unfortunately). But I wanted something so my nipples (Is it okay to say nipples?) wouldn't show through my shirts. Diane told my dad she was far too busy with her classes (yoga, Zumba, and spin) and so my dad had to take me bra shopping. Basically, he just let me pick a bunch of bras off the rack at Walmart and then stood outside the one single dressing room they have in the center of the store yelling, "HOW'S IT GOING IN THERE!?"

The whole experience was so overwhelming I chose the bra by color — pink — not caring much about size, and without trying it on.

When I finally did try on the bra, at home, in the privacy of my bathroom, it took half a roll of Charmin Ultra to fill up the 34-C cups. The final result (after figuring out how to hook it in the back) was the Hunchback of Notre Dame, only in reverse, with the hump on the front.

Olivia walked in and started laughing so hard she cried. Seriously, she was even on the floor of the bathroom and said she may have peed herself. When she stood up, she tried to snap a quick picture of me with her cell phone, but thankfully she'd taken so many selfies that her phone had died. In the end, Olivia traded me the 34-C for an old sports bra of hers, and so my nipple dilemma was solved, and Olivia got a new bra that fit her perfectly.

The other issue Margaret struggles with in the book is religion. She has one Jewish parent and one Christian. My dad and Diane are Episcopalian, so I guess I'm that, but I read if a child has a Jewish mother then the child is automatically Jewish. Are you a Jew, M? (And is it rude to use the word Jew?) I'm not sure if it is or not. The "ish" part confuses me. Why is it Jew-*ish*? I've never heard any other religion use that suffix on the end of their religion: Mormonish? Christianish? Muslimish? Especially since ish means "vagueness," like, when you say "I'll see you at 8-ish," because you just can't commit to 8.

That's it for today. My dad brought home boxes and told me to start packing, which is going to take me a long time because I'm sort of a collector of certain things, although Olivia calls it hoarding.

CWYL,

Willa

P.S. CWYL stands for Chat With You Later. You would probably have figured that out, but I didn't want you to think someone named Cwyl had signed the page.

MARCH 14, 8:42 P.M.

Dear M,

I think Olivia may have been snooping in my room. My diary wasn't in the same spot as where I left it. I distinctly remember putting it underneath the right side of my bed between my mattress and box spring, and when I looked for it tonight, it was almost in the middle. There's a teeny chance it moved on its own because of all the tossing and turning I do when I sleep, but it's doubtful. I guess it's a good thing I don't have much life experience to speak of, or anything to reveal that might get me in trouble. I've never been kissed by a boy and I don't steal, (although sometimes I "borrow" without asking) so there's nothing earth shattering to report.

Here's another thing I wanted to tell you about me ...

Remember how I told you I collect things? Well, I collect two things. The first is erasers. Not the pink rectangle kind you're probably envisioning, but the little kind that are made in China and come in shapes of real things. They can look like food: tiny pizzas, or cheeseburgers, complete with tiny green lettuce and red tomato centers and specs on top to represent sesame seeds on the buns. Or they can be little animals or flowers or stars ... the list is endless, really.

I currently have 4,237 non-duplicate erasers. It's important when you're a serious "curator" like myself not to duplicate. Someday I hope to get into the Guinness Book of World Records. Right now Petra Engels of Germany holds the title. She has 19,571 non-duplicate erasers from all over the world, (but then she's 40 years-old or something, so she's been collecting for a lot longer than I have).

Personally, I think 40 is WAY too old to be collecting kid's erasers, but then Olivia says 6 is too old. Olivia says the only good thing regarding my erasers is that I've finally stopped eating them like I did when I was little. Seriously, for some reason they all smell really sweet and they don't taste half bad. (I probably scarfed down at least two dozen erasers as a kid.)

My dad gave me my first eraser when he was still just Dr. Ted to me and I lived at the orphanage. It was a tiny pepperoni pizza smaller than a dime. He gave it to me right before he told me about my surgery to fix my snarling Chihuahua face. It was a reward, he said, for being so brave. Technically, though, it was a bribe not a reward, because he gave it to me before anything happened. For something to be a reward it has to come

AFTER the event. A bribe happens before it.

He brought me a new eraser every time he came to the orphanage to work on my teeth. Unfortunately, none of the erasers ever made it OUT of the orphanage, because, like I told you, those things smell delish! But that's how I started my love affair with erasers.

The nice thing about having an eraser collection is that they're easy to store. My dad bought me tons of blue plastic tackle boxes, the kind with shelves that fold out, and so it's super easy for me to organize my erasers by theme and color. One time, when Olivia was mad at me, (I'm referring to one specific time of the many times she's been mad) she opened all of my tackle boxes and dumped all of my erasers onto the floor of my closet. It took me a week to re-categorize them, and I never did find my favorite Hello Kitty one.

FYI: I am NOT a Hello Kitty girl in any way, shape or form, and have never so much as worn a Hello Kitty headband or owned a Hello Kitty keychain. But every self-respecting collector needs at least one Hello Kitty eraser in his or her collection in order to be classified a seasoned professional.

My other collection is calendars, but it's a small collection compared to my erasers.

I have exactly twelve calendars, one for every year of my life since the day you ~~ditched~~... umm ... I mean, BROUGHT me to Children's Home Society, but I have each month individually tacked to my wall in orderly fashion, so it seems as if I have about a million. In reality, it comes out to 148 months, but some of the months are really small because they were cut from the pages of pocket calendars. Whenever something good happens to me I write it down in secret code on the day, so for the most part it looks like just a bunch of tiny numbers. Obviously, I don't need to write things down to remember, but sometimes it's nice to have a visual reminder my life isn't always bad, and if I can look at the calendar and see the tiny numbers, my mind will stay in present time, reaffirming something GOOD happened.

What good, you might ask?

1. Like getting an A on my English test and then NOT getting hit in the head with someone's apple core, half-eaten baloney sandwich, or Fig Newton in the lunchroom at

school. (Note to parents: Kids do not like Fig Newtons!)

2. Having my dad take me out for ice cream because he knows Diane is PMSing and I'm an easy target.

3. Getting two new, hot-off-the-press erasers (because Diane vacuumed up three.)

4. Being allowed to have cereal for dinner.

5. Being allowed to have cereal for dinner. (I know I already mentioned this, but if you ever ate Diane's cooking you would know why it's worth repeating.)

I considered giving up my calendars now that I have this diary, but I don't think I will. It's nice to have a visual reminder of the good. Also, if I ever give you this diary in person, I'd lose the physical link. Does that make sense?

Until next time,

Willa, your daughter.

(Does the word "daughter" make you feel weird? Now that I see it on the page, I realize it looks kind of stupid.)

MARCH 20, 5:58 P.M.

Dear M,

Today is the first day of spring, and let me tell you, I am SOOO over the cold in Chicago. Not that I'm looking forward to the heat of California, but it would be nice not to have goosebumps every day. (Olivia says those are not goosebumps, they are my breasts.)

So far, the packing and stuff is going pretty well for our big move, but Olivia is becoming a major drama queen and insisting she is NOT moving because she can't possibly LIVE without all of her friends. Yesterday, to get her to quit her whining, Diane pointed out that maybe Olivia will be discovered by a talent agent and have a chance at stardom.

The ruse worked. Olivia definitely feels better, and now she's going around telling all of her friends that she'll be starring in a new reality show on E! based on her life and called "She's All That."

Say what? As if!

Olivia has no idea "She's All That" was the name of a movie that came out in 1999 starring Freddie Prinze Jr. and Rachael Leigh Cook, where a high school jock (Freddie Prinze) makes a bet he can turn an unattractive girl (Rachael Leigh Cook) into the school's prom queen.

I've seen the movie twice now and it's pretty good, but I have to say I have some issues with ugly-duckling-turned-swan movies where the producers just throw a pair of glasses on a pre-existing swan (and maybe a lumpy sweater or something that even a pretty girl would look bad in) and then everyone goes all bananas at the end of the movie about the amazing transformation just because the girl has taken off her glasses and is wearing a cute dress and has her hair in an updo for a change. Seems to me it would be more believable if they started out with an ugly girl and just made her less ugly by the end of the movie.

Not to change the subject or anything, but did you have a lot of slumber parties when you were my age? (Or did you call them "sleepovers?") Olivia has had loads of them, but I've never even had a single one. I'm not saying that so you'll feel sorry for me, because, seriously, I never really wanted one before now. When you grow up in an orphanage with hundreds of screaming kids and are forced to sleep sometimes three to a bed because of overcrowding, believe me, you get your fill of slumber parties!

The reason I'm even bringing it up is because my dad said I could have a going away slumber party. I told him I'd think about it and let him know, but to be honest, I don't really have anyone to invite. I'm not saying I have NO friends. I have a few, but it's not as if I have one single BEST friend.

My closest friend — emotionally speaking, not geographically; there are no other kids on my street — is probably Akshay. Akshay is new to our school, and the day we met he was on the INSIDE of his locker pounding for someone to let him out. His locker is right below mine, so I was the obvious choice. Akshay is from India, and one of his legs is shorter than the other so he wears a shoe with two extra inches of rubber on the bottom of it.

"Birds of a feather," as they say, and so we became the unofficial Nerd Patrol, along with Georgie, who is 15, but who has Downs, and so he's in our grade because he kept getting held back.

Now can you see my problem about the slumber party/sleepover?

My dad would probably have a minor issue about my sleepover friends being boys and Diane would have a MAJOR issue! Not because they are boys — necessarily, but because they are boys who are ... How do I say this? ... (And I'm struggling with how Diane sees them, not how I see them, because I just see them as regular boys: funny, a little weird, and with that strange boy smell.)

funky

The fact is, Diane is one of those people who is so out of touch she still uses mean words like "retard" for the mentally challenged and "colored" for anyone with skin darker than copy paper. Diane's standard defense regarding her blatant racism is that she's from West Virginia where the population is over 94% Caucasian. Her retard comments, on the other hand, have no such excuse and shows what an intellectual moron she is. Honestly, I don't know what my dad sees in her!

Now that I see it all written in black and white, I know my party is never going to happen.

Maybe I'll make some friends in California and then I can have a sleepover. Is a sleepover even fun? Or am I making a big deal out of it and it's going to turn out the same way as my tiramisu experience? (Tiramisu is a fancy dessert I kept hearing about for years that my dad would never let me order off the menu because he said it was too expensive. Then finally, on my 11th birthday, my dad let me order tiramisu, and it was a total letdown! I'm not kidding, a scoop of plain vanilla is WAY better than tiramisu.)

I have to go now. I'm writing this before dinner and my dad's calling me to say dinner is ready. Tonight is taco night, and I LOVE ME SOME TACOS!!

Willita

P.S. "Willita" means little Willa in Spanish.

MARCH 25 4:43 P.M.

Dear M,

Would you believe it if I told you I can remember what you smell like? (Does that make me a creepy McCreepster?)

I know it sounds farfetched since I was only one when you left me, but I can. I remember you smelled like a combination of flowers, grass, oranges, and vanilla.

I'm not saying that at one I knew exactly the names of each certain scent, that would be pretty remarkable, but as I got old enough to identify smells I added them to my list until eventually I figured out it probably wasn't your regular human smell, that it must have been your perfume. (And can someone please tell me why some people's regular smell is like Campbell's Chicken Noodle Soup while other people smell fresh like powder even at the end of the day?)

Finally, today, after all of these years, I think I know the name of your perfume. It's called PINK, and it's by Victoria's Secret. The reason I say this is because today we had a substitute in my math class, Mrs. Edelstein, and she smelled EXACTLY like you. The similarity ends there, because Mrs. Edelstein is a "robust woman," as my dad would say, and she has gray hair and a mole on her chin with a long hair growing out of it.

As soon as Mrs. Edelstein walked by my desk her perfume washed over me and I was immediately transported back in time to our last few minutes together. Not just because of my H-SAM either, but because the sense of smell is our strongest connection to memory. (From what I understand, it's because the pathways in our nose are a shortcut to the amygdala and the hippocampus in our brains, two areas strongly linked to emotion and memory.)

You held me against your chest, super tight, so tight I could feel the softness of the fabric of your shirt against my cheek and hear the heavy beating of your heart against my ear, the way it thumped harder with each step you took up the stairs.

When Diane heard me tell the doctors at the University what I'm telling you, she said I was making it up. No child that young could possibly remember something that happened when they were only one, she told them. But I swear, I really remember! I remember it as if it happened yesterday, or this morning. I can see the sad expression on your face, the tears tracing a pattern down your cheeks. I can feel the pressure of the kiss from your lips on my forehead, before you handed me to the woman who answered the door.

I'd be lying if I told you I remember the words you said to the woman as you handed me over to her, but I remember the FEELINGS. The sorrow rolling off you so thick I felt it cloak me like a blanket.

And I remember after you left I cried and cried for hours. Cried so hard I couldn't catch my breath, and so I hiccupped and gulped for air while snot ran down my nose and onto the front of my shirt. I remember nobody could seem to calm me, not by rocking me or patting my back. Not even the offer of the lollipop. Until, finally, they gave up trying and just put me in a metal crib where eventually I cried myself to sleep, but starting over all again the next morning when I realized you weren't coming back to get me.

The doctors at the University think the emotional trauma is what brought on the H-SAM. That I might have remained a normal kid — relative to memory, anyway — if not for going through what I did.

Looking back, I know they must be right because I don't remember anything prior to that day. Not the house we lived in. Or my first birthday party (assuming I had one.) I can't remember what my father looked like, or if I even had one. I mean, OBVIOUSLY, I had a father ... It's not as if you were Mary the Virgin and I was your modern-day girl version of Jesus. What I mean to say is I don't remember if my father was in our lives. I've tried to concentrate and go back in time, but no matter what I do, I can't seem to go back any farther than that day on the front sidewalk of the CHSC.

Can I ask you a question? (I mean ANOTHER question. I don't know about you, but I hate it when someone says to me "Can I ask you a question?" because they have already asked one. What they need to say is "Can I ask you another question besides this one?")

Did you turn back around after you handed me over and walked down the steps? Or did you just keep walking?

Willa

APRIL 1, 4:59 P.M.

Dear M,

I haven't written to you in a while because I got in trouble and so I've been really bummed and not in the mood to write. Plus, each passing day is one day closer to moving, so there's that to contend with.

First off though, you are NOT going to believe why I'm in trouble! Are you ready for this? (And I swear, this is not an April Fool's joke.) I actually got in trouble for shaving my underarms. FOR SHAVING MY UNDERARMS!! How lame is that? Honestly, M., you would have thought I shaved the neighbor's Persian cat if you heard the ruckus it caused around here.

This is how it happened:

The short story is I used Olivia's Daisy razor and gave a quick swipe under my arms, and voila! Smooth underarms.

The long story is that knowing I might have to wear a bathing suit in just a matter of weeks, and also knowing there was no way I'd let anyone see the long, black, and totally gross hairs under my arms, I decided I needed to take some action. The rest was pretty easy. I got in the shower, soaped until I had a good lather, and then swiped. One pass under each arm was all it took because even though the hair was long, it wasn't like it was a forest or anything.

Well, when Olivia went to take a shower, she

saw my underarm hairs lodged in the blades of her razor and she totally freaked out. I mean, like, she was screaming as if she found a skinned animal pelt stuck on the razor's edge instead of just a few of my underarm hairs. Then she became a total tattletale, yelling, "MOMMM!!" So of course Diane came running to the bathroom expecting to see something really heinous and instead only sees Olivia holding a razor with a few hairs that may or may not have actually been a couple of threads from a sweater or something. Seriously, Diane had to put on her reading glasses just to see what Olivia was talking about.

Then Olivia started insisting I should be GROUNDED. Not only for going against the rule of No Shaving Underarms Until Marriage, (or maybe prom) but also for using her razor without asking permission. (Which she would never in a million years give me anyway.)

Diane was pretty mad and she droned on with some lecture how rules were "in place for a reason," but when I asked her to give me just one reasonable explanation why a twelve-year-old with Rapunzel length hairs under her arms should NOT be allowed to shave, she couldn't come up with a single one. But Olivia was like a "dog with a bone," as the saying goes, and she would not let it go. She even followed her mom down the hallway harping about how I needed to be grounded to teach me a lesson about rule breaking, which is a hoot because Olivia breaks the rules every day.

Diane told her she'd think of a FITTING PUNISHMENT for me and went to get ready for her Pilates class, but Olivia was hot on her trail, still nagging about it. Finally, when Diane was in her bedroom and thought I was out of earshot and couldn't hear, she said, "For goodness' sake, Olivia! Grounding Willa would be punishment for ME, not HER. The girl never leaves the house as it is. If I had my way Willa would be out of the house MORE often, not less!"

I'll admit it, what Diane said hurt my feelings, but then it wouldn't be the first time. Diane tends to be a speak-before-you-think kind of person according to my dad.

M, I wasn't kidding when I said you should marry my dad so he can kick Diane to the curb. He's way too nice for her. He's not buff or anything, and he's pretty nerdish looking with his glasses, and he has this knobby knee thing going on, but he's a really hard worker and he always sees the best in everyone. He's the kind of guy who always roots for the underdog (which means he's usually on the side of the losing team).

I'm going to close for now. I'm in the process of categorizing my eraser collection before I box them up for the move, and it's turning out to be harder than I imagined. (Would you categorize erasers shaped as ice cream as dessert or dairy?)

Until next time,

Willa

APRIL 5, 3:39 P.M.

Dear M,

Is kissing something you need to practice first before you try it, or is it like learning how to skip, where you watch someone do it a couple times and then you just go for it and hope you get it right?

The reason I ask is because Olivia insists you have to practice kissing or you take the risk of smashing a boy's face with your lips. When I asked her where on earth I'd find someone to practice with, (it's not as if the boys are lining up to hang out with me) she told me you don't practice with a REAL person, but instead you practice with a ripe plum.

Yes, a ripe plum! Do you think she was punking me? It wouldn't be the first time.

Like that one Christmas Eve the year I was 7.

It was after Dad and Diane had gone to bed. Olivia came to my room to tell me Santa Clause was stuck in our chimney and he needed my help. She even got me the step stool from the garage so I could climb UP inside the chimney from the fireplace and help dislodge Santa.

As you can guess, Santa was NOT inside the chimney, and I wound up getting in trouble for ruining my new Christmas pajamas from all that soot.

Or the Easter four years ago, when Olivia told me the Easter bunny had taken one look at my face while I was asleep and decided I was too ugly to deserve a basket. She told me the bunny decided to give my basket to HER so she could have two, the extra one as a reward for her superior beauty. (Her stunt backfired because Dad made Olivia give me half of the candy in her basket as punishment for being so mean.)

So now you know why I take everything Olivia says "with a grain of salt," which means to maintain a degree of skepticism about its truthfulness.

I asked Olivia if I could substitute another fruit because we didn't have any plums, ripe or otherwise, but she said no, it had to be a ripe plum because they had some squish to them and real lips have squish.

We're not a big plum family, (we like apples, oranges, bananas, and the occasional pear) so I had to ask my dad if he'd pick me up some plums from the grocery store. He asked me what kind, and I said I had no idea. I started to say "Anything that looks KISSABLE," but I stopped before I got the word out, and I changed it to EDIBLE, instead. I also told him it ties into my science project, and so he needed to get me an assortment and to buy at least half a dozen. (I wasn't sure if I'd turn out to be a good kisser and maybe I'd need more than one or two in order to get the hang of things.)

You might not know this M, but there is a regular U.N. when it comes to plums! Seriously, I can now say I'm prepared to kiss a boy not only from several of the major countries in Europe, (with emphasis on Italian and French) but also Japan and China. I know one would think the Italian and French boys would be the best kissers, with all the hype about them in the movies, (assuming their plums have some correlation to their kissing ability) but I'd have to say, from my plum experience, I think I'm going to try to find Japanese boys.

Here's what I found:

1. European plums are oblong and firm. So firm that they don't have a lot of give to them and so they don't make for a great kissing experience, (but they did have a nice purple color to them, very similar to real lips.)

2. Chinese plums (at least the ones my dad bought) are yellow and heart shaped. The color part didn't bother me, but I had to do this weird pucker thing with my lips in order for them to fit on the side of the plum because of the odd shape, and so it was really awkward.

3. Japanese plums are fragrant, round, and a purple-black color. (Again, this is not a concrete science. I'm only going with my limited experience to the plums I tried.) They respond well to a medium lip press and will spring back, but beware of a firm press, or the skin will split leaving you with no choice but to eat the plum, which has a

wonderful sweet flavor.

***It's worth noting, regardless of place of origin, there are many unique and special plums that defy stereotype, appearing in different shapes and colors than their plum brethren. All of these plums are special in God's eyes.

And so now I may be ready to kiss a boy when the option is presented to me. (Unfortunately I also have to come up with an extra credit science project involving plums, because I don't like to lie to my dad, and plus, he spent a fortune on fruit.)

Until next time,

Willa

APRIL 9, 7:07 P.M.

Dear M,

Tick tock tick tock.

Time is flying by way too quickly! In just two weeks I'll be a "California kid," as my dad says. Well, you know what? I don't want to be a California kid. I want to be a Chicago kid!

Here's what I like about Chicago:

1. Chicago has great public transportation. I've been riding the public bus by myself since I was 7. (Although, now that I think about it, 7 seems awfully young to be riding a bus alone. Do you think my family was hoping to get rid of me?? If so, their devious plan was unsuccessful.)

2. Chicago has the best hot dogs and pizza in the whole world. (I don't know if that's a statistical fact, but I'm willing to bet the

rest of the world would agree if they tasted our dogs and our pie.)

3. We have a large body of water that looks like an ocean, but without the man-eating sharks and the drying effect on your skin from of all that nasty salt.

4. We have animals galore! And by animals I mean we have Bears, Bulls, Cubs, Wildcats and Blackhawks, and they play at two awesome fields, Wrigley and Soldier.

5. Unlike California, we actually have 4 seasons! Sure, one of them sucks dirty socks (winter, obviously) and summer can

get pretty miserable with the heat and humidity, but spring and fall are super amazing, and so it all evens out in the end.

There's a lot of other things I like about Chicago. Like how the night skyline can look like a painted picture, and the great art museums; how you can go back time after time and yet always see something new; and the awesome libraries, filled with as many books as you see in those Harry Potter movies where the books go from floor to ceiling and so you have to use ladders to get the ones higher up, and with staircases that curve and twist, with banisters so shiny and polished you see your reflection. Plus, the library has the most awesome smell!

You know what, M? Someone should come out with a perfume that smells like a library. You know the smell I'm talking about. It's sort of musty, which I know is actually cellulose decay, so that could be the base note, and mixed with a slightly sweet smell like bee's wax, which could be the middle, or what's referred to as the "heart note." The top note, that's the part of the fragrance that fades the quickest, could be chocolate chip cookie.

Not that any library I've ever been in smells like chocolate chip cookies, but if I'm making up a library fragrance, I think that would make a nice blend. Don't you agree? What would we call our fragrance? What about "COMPENDIUM"? In case you don't remember from school, compendium means a concise compilation of knowledge. (As I told you earlier, I'm terrible at math, but I love to read, so I have a pretty good vocabulary for someone my age. I know it doesn't seem that way so far, but that's because I don't want you to think I'm showing off by using big words.)

Now that I think about it, I don't think I've "put my best foot forward", as the saying goes. I'm vastly more intelligent than I've let on. Okay, so maybe "vastly" is overstating things, but I'm certainly more intelligent than everyone in my family except for my dad. Seriously, I am waayyyy smarter than Olivia, and I'm willing to bet my I.Q. is a lot higher than Diane's, who, I'll have you know, insists the word "often" is pronounced off-ten, when everyone with half a brain knows the T is silent and the word is pronounced offin. (If you ever forget, remember often rhymes with soften.)

Do you know what the longest word in the dictionary is? Let me give you a hint, it is

NOT supercalifragilisticexpialidocious, regardless of what Olivia says. The longest word in the dictionary is actually pneumonoultramicroscopicsilicovolcanoconiosis and it's a lung disease you get from inhaling very small silica particles from a volcano.

I actually thought I had it once, the disease — after I learned about it, but come to find out, pneumonoultramicroscopicsilicovolcanoconiosis mimics bronchitis.

I'm going to admit something to you now and I hope you won't think less of me for it. I'm pretty sure I'm a hypochondriac. A hypochondriac, just as a refresher, is a person with an unwarranted fear they have a serious disease.

Does anyone else in our family suffer from that? My dad says not to worry, and it might somehow tie in with my OCD, but, Hello!!

How can I NOT worry when I have no idea what may be lurking in my DNA?

These are the most common genetic things I worry about:

Cystic fibrosis

Muscular dystrophy

Hemophilia

Neurofibromatosis

Polycystic kidney disease

Sickle-cell anemia (And so, yeah, I know that 80% of people with sickle-cell are of African descent, but that validates my point, that, because I know NOTHING about my DNA, I could, in this very second, be developing sickle-cell anemia.)

Tay-Sachs (Any chance I'm French Canadian or an Ashkenazi Jew? If not, I should be okay. Especially since if I had Tay-Sachs I'd be dead now because Tay-Sachs kids don't live past the age of 4.)

I think I need to call it quits for now. I just noticed a suspicious-looking mole on the inside of my left arm that might be pre-cancerous and I should probably have my dad look at. I know, it sounds as if I am totally making it up, but seriously, M, this thing has some irregular margins. If I do have cancer, it wouldn't be your fault necessarily, because non-melanoma skin cancer is from sun exposure, and not genetically transferred.

Yours in good health, (hopefully)

Willa

APRIL 10, 6:36 P.M.

Dear M,

Great news!! I do NOT have skin cancer. Come to find out, it was a burnt Frosted Flake crumb that got stuck to the inside of my arm. You know how sometimes Frosted Flakes have a couple of burnt flakes at the bottom of the bag? Well, I guess I got one in my bowl, and when I went to drink the milk, the flake fell on my arm. Because the flake was sticky from the milk, it glued itself to my arm, and so it only LOOKED like a crusty skin cancer nodule.

I do have another serious health question to ask you though, and I hope you don't think it's too personal. It's about your zits.

Say what?

I mean, what I want to know is, did you have zits?

I get them sometimes, but when I asked Olivia how to get rid of them, she said she knows nothing about pimples or their treatment, as she has never had a single one! Which is a load of malarky because I found a tube of acne cream hidden inside Olivia's Kotex holder. I've heard teenaged girls like to hide stuff like cigarettes inside their Kotex holders, but not Olivia (who doesn't smoke). Instead, Olivia has to hide anything that proves she's an actual imperfect human, instead of a spray-tanned, plasticized, Barbiezilla. She also hid a tube of something called Vagasil behind the rolls of toilet paper under our bathroom sink. I have no idea what it is or what it's for, and for that matter, I don't want to know!

So, about your zits ... or do you call them "spots"? I know British people call them spots and I still don't know your country of origin, so maybe you call them something else. Maybe you're a hoity-toity kind of a lady and you call them "blemishes." Or maybe you grew up in the Appalachia mountains of Tennessee and you call them carbuncles, or furuncles, or caruncles, or pustules.

I think it's best for this conversation if we just call them pimples.

What I want to know, specifically, is did you have a face full of them, like full-blown acne? Or did you just get one or two of them from time to time? So far, I only get one every once in a while, but I need to be prepared for a full blown, double pepperoni, pizza face. I haven't had the best luck in the looks department, between my cleft lip and those extra teeth, so as you can appreciate, I need to have some sort of game plan (short of wearing a ski mask for all of my teenage years).

I'm trying not to obsess over it, but obsession is sort of my nature if you haven't guessed by now, (hence my diagnosis, OBSESSIVE COMPULSIVE DISORDER, in addition to my H-SAM.) I got the double whammy from the doctors when they diagnosed me with OCD and H-SAM at the same time. I gotta say, the OCD I saw coming, especially after I saw the movie "As Good As It Gets" with Jack Nicholson and Helen Hunt. I totally related to the way Jack's character, Melvin, always has to have his silverware just right before he eats, and how he doesn't like to step on the cracks in the sidewalk, but I'm not kidding when I tell you the H-SAM diagnosis totally threw me. Come to find out, it is NOT a normal thing to remember every day of your life with perfect recall.

I don't think I've fully explained the full misery of H-SAM, so let me try to explain it another way this time.

Once a memory surfaces and sticks to my consciousness, H-SAM can be compared to what happens when someone puts a broken record on a turntable. The needle sticks in the groove of the record and the song repeats itself over and over and over, until finally you unstick the needle and it moves on to the next song, or in my case, a different memory. If the needle is stuck on a fun happy song, you'll dance around for the first few versions of that one song, singing and laughing and having a good time, until eventually you've had more than enough rainbows and shining stars, magic dragons, and yellow daffodils, and you want to break that stupid record in half.

I could probably do the same thing, the singing and laughing part, for the first few renditions of a memory, until I'd had my fill of all that syrupy sweetness. (Not to mention all the sha na na's. For some reason, all those old happy songs have a bunch of sha na na's in common.)

But here's the kicker when it comes to my life.

I don't have the happy memories. I don't have the rainbows and the shining stars, the magic dragons, and the yellow daffodils. And I've never had a single sha na na moment in my entire life.

Instead ...

I've had unimaginable heartbreak.

I've had soul crushing abandonment.

I've had extreme loneliness and unfathomable hurt.

And so my record sticks constantly on the sad songs, the ones with lyrics about lost love, and broken dreams, shattered hearts, (and maybe a stormy night, like, in Georgia, or somewhere).

Please don't think I'm trying to blame you or anything. You probably thought I'd get adopted pretty quickly, even with my messed up face, and by a halfway decent family. This is Chicago, right? There are over 9.4 million people in the Chicago metropolitan area and almost 13 million in the state of Illinois. You'd think the chances of me getting out of that orphanage as a baby would have been pretty strong.

Holy Moly! I just re-read today's entry. Man, I need to take a chill pill. What a sap. I'd erase the entire entry, but believe it or not, I don't have a single rubber eraser, and the one on the end of this pencil is broken.

How's that for irony? I have over 4,000 erasers and not one to erase with. But using one of my novelty erasers would be like playing backyard baseball with Mark McGwire's 70th Home Run Ball from his 1998 season, so I guess it has to stay.

Just disregard everything past, "Here's the kicker when it comes to my life."

Yours in utter humiliation,

Willa

APRIL 15, 8:48 P.M.

Dear M,

I know it's been awhile, but I fell into a black abyss of self-pity for a few days after I last wrote and I didn't want to bring that sort of negativity into your life.

I mean, WHO needs THAT, right?

But I'm better now. Especially since my dad and I had father/daughter night and went to Mickey D's where my dad let me order anything I wanted, unlike Diane, who makes me order a lame and basically tasteless Kid's Meal. (FYI, I had a Double Quarter Pounder with Cheese, a large fry. And by that I mean a large ORDER OF FRIES — I don't mean to imply I just had one single gigantic one. I also had a large vanilla shake.)

I wanted to order a McCafé Frappé Caramel,

but my dad said it has caffeine and would "jack me up higher than a prom skirt in May" which I could tell he immediately regretted saying because his face turned all red and he sort of choked on his Pico Guacamole with 100% Pure Beef 1/4 lb. Patty Burger.

What do you think that means? That prom skirt remark? I've never been to prom, and as far as I can tell from pictures, the girls all wear dresses, not skirts. I asked my dad to explain, but he said "Forget it. I shouldn't have said that."

I love father/daughter night with my dad.

 Special

Especially since Olivia never gets to have one, but that's Olivia's fault because Olivia won't eat fast food, and my dad says there is no way he is taking a 15-year-old to "Chez Shi-Shi Fa La La." I don't think that's really the name of the restaurant, I think my dad was just trying to make a point.

He's offered to have father/daughter night with her doing other things besides eating, but so far Olivia has nixed every idea. He once suggested bowling, which got him a "Bowling!! Are you freakin' kidding me?? And wear those nasty gross shoes filled with other peoples' toe-jam?"

Or a movie with just the two of them...

"GO TO THE MOVIES ON A DATE WITH MY FATHER??!!! WHAT KIND OF A FREAK WOULD DO THAT?? WHAT IF MY FRIENDS SAW US?? I'D BE THE LAUGHINGSTOCK OF THE SCHOOL!!"

My dad pointed out it would hardly be considered a "date," and so he took ME to the movies instead, and we got to see "Guardians of the Galaxy" in 3-D and had a really good time.

Fun!

He even offered to take her to Sky Zone Trampoline Park, but she said that was just a combo version of the bowling thing AND the movies because the trampoline mat was covered in sweaty feet excrement and that by going with just the two of them it made Dad look like a perv who drives a white panel van.

So as you can see, things did get better for me after we last "spoke." I told my dad what I told you, about not having very many good memories to hold onto, and he said, "What am I? Chopped liver?" using one of my fries as a pointer for emphasis. His question wasn't literal, obviously. He was using an old-fashioned saying meaning someone feels they're overlooked. The saying came about because chopped liver was traditionally served as a side dish years ago, rather than as the main course, and so the liver got "overlooked." (As well as it should have because liver is totally DISGUSTING!!)

My dad was right. (He usually is.) I do have some good memories of our time together with just the two of us. But is it greedy, M, to want more?

I want to have memories of doing stuff with kids my age. Of going bowling with a big group of friends and wearing those clown-looking bowling shoes while someone snaps selfies of us. Memories of seeing a movie with a BFF, or maybe even a boy. And it would make a super cool memory if he tried to hold my hand, which I probably wouldn't let him do anyway, because I have really sweaty hands, and he'd probably think I was gross and wouldn't ever want to see me again. But still, that would be a great memory to have, of a boy TRYING to hold my hand.

PERFECT DAY!

Another thing that happened after dinner with my dad is that now Diane is trying to be nicer to me. Olivia says it's because my dad has bribed her with a promise to remodel the kitchen in the new house. I don't know why Diane would need a new kitchen. Diane doesn't cook. A microwave on top of a TV tray and Diane is pretty much good to go.

Here is an example of Diane being nicer to me.

April 12, 7:59 a.m. (before school)

"Willa, DEAR, you're wearing THAT to school, AGAIN? Wouldn't you like to dress like a girl for a change?" (I know, it's not that nice, but Diane never adds words of endearments when she speaks to me, so it was definitely an improvement.)

April 13, 3:04 p.m. (getting picked up from school)

"How was your day, Willa? Did you manage to make it through lunch without getting hit in the head with a soggy peanut butter and jelly sandwich?" (Diane doesn't usually ask how my day was, so her interest in me was a shocker.)

April 14, 9:01 p.m. (in the hallway)

"Goodnight, Willa. Hopefully, tomorrow will be a better day for you." (That was a double positive. Diane actually said goodnight, and she wished a better day for me — even though it was NOT a bad day, Diane just assumed it was since most of them are.)

M, as you can see, there is a definite uptick trend happening in Diane's treatment of me. Olivia said Diane is working on a points system, and that X amount of points equals X amounts of add-ons to Diane's new kitchen. So far Diane has earned herself Frigidaire brand appliances, but Olivia says her mom is hoping for Wolf, which is the top of the line.

If I write and tell you Diane is tucking me into bed at night and reading me bedtime stories, you'll know she's earned herself a chef's Commercial Kitchen.

Willa

APRIL 17, 5:16 P.M.

Dear M,

Do you have any brothers or sisters? If so, how many? I think it would be really cool to know if I have aunts and uncles and cousins.

There is not much of an extended family in the Shisbey lineage. My dad was an only child, and his parents died before he adopted me. Diane is also an only child, but her parents are alive and kicking, (although I did recently hear Diane complain to my dad and say he was a "lucky duck" because he didn't have "parents still living and meddling in their lives.")

I think it would be fun to have a brother or sister. I mean, like a REAL sibling, one who actually liked me, and not Olivia who has hated me since the day my dad first brought me home.

Did I tell you that the first day I arrived Olivia locked me in the closet and flushed the key down the toilet? My dad totally freaked and kept yelling "Don't worry, Willa, I'LL SAVE YOU!!" And he was all dramatic-like with the "I'll save you," when he could just as easily have said, "I'll have you out in a jiffy," because all it took was a screwdriver inserted into the keyhole to get me out. Plus, it was the coat closet, and so I was in there with the winter coats, and it was super cozy with all of those puffy down jackets smooshed against me.

Here is the thing about Olivia.

Olivia is like one of those deadly beautiful flowers, the Adenium Obesum, let's say, the second most lethal flower on the planet, with her flawless skin and her dimples, her big blue eyes, and her silky blond hair. Like the flower, Olivia looks like something you'd want an entire bouquet of, a whole vase filled with her fragrance and loveliness. But looks can be deceiving, and like the flower, the nectar that oozes from Olivia's pretty core could kill an elephant.

Olivia isn't ALWAYS mean. She can "play nice" if she wants to, which is almost as disgusting to watch as when she's in full-blown maniacal meltdown.

When Olivia wants her way she uses this fake sweet voice and she bats those eyelash extensions so it looks as if there's a dying butterfly on her cheek flapping its wings for the last time. Guys especially fall for this mockery. I've actually seen guys trip over each other to get close to Olivia when she starts with her, "Oh, MY, I am just SO thirsty!

Whatever shall I do?" Honestly, it's all I can do to keep from vomiting.

Then, of course, the boys all run to do her bidding, getting her a soda, or whatever, and for a couple minutes she'll be all, like, "Well, I do declare, aren't you just the nicest thing EVER?" before wrapping them in silk made from her spit and setting them aside to eat later. (That's a spider reference. And I'm kidding about the "I do declare" statement. She usually just says a simple "Thanks.")

To give Olivia some credit, she does refer to me as her sister, but she always has to clarify it and say I'm her "adopted sister," and then she gives them some ridiculous Oliver Twist-inspired story about how SHE saw me in a basket on the steps of the Children's Home Society of Chicago and INSISTED that my parents immediately adopt me, "the poor hideous motherless creature," because in

Olivia's words, "If not us, then who?" meaning of course no one else would want me. Which, I guess, now that I think about it, she was 100% correct.

As you know, M, there was no basket involved, and I'm willing to go out on a limb and say you had some sort of conversation with someone at the Home first, and maybe filled out paperwork or something, and so they were expecting us that day.

Maybe if we ever meet in person you could bring pictures of ~~your~~ ... my family. And then if you're comfortable with it, introduce me to them. You wouldn't have to say I'm your daughter, if it's a secret. Instead, you could say I'm a friend of a friend, or maybe you could tell them I'm part of a Big Sister Program, and I'm your Little Sister. That way, if we went out for an ice cream or to the zoo, it would make a good "cover" and no one would be the wiser.

I was part of the Big Sister Program for a while when I was at the orphanage, but they nixed the program when my Big Sister, Darlene, left me inside a Chuck E. Cheese's for over 3 hours while she went to her boyfriend's house to party. I didn't mind. I didn't like her much anyway and she left me with plenty of tokens to play games, but since I was only 4 it had some legal consequences, and so they had to scratch the program for fear of potential lawsuits.

Here's the move update:

My room is pretty much packed and in moving boxes stacked inside something called a Pod parked in our driveway. Pod is just shorthand for "cargo trailer," only it's nicely painted and with big red lettering that says PODS, (which, if I'm being a stickler for grammatical correctness, is incorrect, as it is one SINGLE Pod, not two or more, and so it should read "Pod" — singular.) Unless of course Pods is the name of the company, not the product itself, in which case Pods with an S is correct.

Olivia has yet to pack a thing. She said she "Just can't bear it!" and she's not moving, and can she live with either Bethany or Brittany? Or maybe she meant her other friend Britney, (the names sound the same but the spelling is different.)

UGH!!!! I'm doing it again. And by IT, I mean where I get on some weird tangent and all of a sudden I'm critiquing everyone's spelling or pronunciation, or obsessing about the misuse of apostrophes.

Quick, yell "Squirrel!" so I'll chase off in a different direction.

Is it any wonder I don't have friends? Honestly, sometimes even I don't want to have to hang out with me because of how annoying I can be.

I have to go now. It's time to alphabetize the canned goods in the pantry. (I am SO kidding! As a confession, I really do like to have all the labels facing OUT in an orderly manner, but I'm perfectly fine if the corn is to the right of the green beans and left of the peas.)

Yours in perpetual weirdness,

Willa

APRIL 28, 3:19 P.M.

Dear M,

You are NOT going to believe what happened! I'd tell you to guess, but that would be ridiculous because there are way too many variables and so it's pretty close to a statistical impossibility you'd guess correctly without giving you multiple choices.

But I digress.

Anyway, today my dad took me to Children's Home Society so I could give them my forwarding address in person in case you came looking for me, and so I could say goodbye to the staff. At first, I wasn't sure why he wanted me to say goodbye to them. I already said goodbye when I left there 7 years ago. Plus, most of the staff who helped care for me no longer work there.

The way my dad said it, "Say your goodbyes," it sounded sort of ominous, so it got me to thinking there might be something he wasn't telling me. Like, maybe he thought I'd NEVER get another chance to go back and see them. (As in, it's lights out, señorita or the Grim Reaper was getting ready to knock on my door or something.)

Then my dad reeled me back to reality and he said that what he MEANT was it would be the last time I'd be able to go for "a while," and so it might be nice to visit and have "closure."

It was insane, M, because the memories started firing at me as soon as I stepped through the door:

October 26, ten years ago. Two years, eight months old, and a budding artist. I stuck a purple crayon (Vivid Violet and without the paper sleeve) up my nose and tried to color with it. It took the staff three hours of unsuccessful fishing before the trip to the ER.

The nice doctor removed that one, plus a yellow one (Canary, WITH the sleeve and covered in snot) he found stuck up the other nostril. That event happened in my Barney the Dinosaur days. I loved drawing pictures of Barney. Although the ones done by hand always came out better than the ones done by nose.

Labor Day, September 6, the following year. Clear as day I recalled getting spanked for lifting Myrna's flowered dress. Myrna worked the 11-7 shift and she looked perpetually pregnant. The reason I lifted her dress was because I wanted to see up-close where babies came from. I was gunning for her stomach, but now that I'm older I can see how my actions may have been misunderstood when I tried to pull down her faded granny-panties in order to better see her belly.

The new supervisor, Mrs. McNair, said Myrna no longer works there. Hasn't worked there for ages. That she got gastric bypass six years ago and lost fifty pounds and now she's married and living in Florida in a new condominium.

Mrs. McNair gave us a tour to show me the improvements. And boy, have things changed since I was there! I guess there's a lot of new laws on what you can and can't do in an orphanage. Like how they can no longer have three kids sleep in one bed, so instead they have triple-stacked bunk beds in the rooms. If we had that when I was there I would have insisted on the bottom bunk, because it has to be a pain in the butt to climb down from three stories up just to pee at night.

Also, she said they can't have girls and boys taking baths together, regardless of how young they are. Too much potential for shenanigans. And speaking of shenanigans, that brought back the memory of when I was three years, two months, and nine days old, and I accidentally let loose a butt burp that started off a chain reaction of underwater nuclear proportions when the other two kids in the tub with me followed my lead. (Ha! That was funny. It was totally gross, but funny.)

There was a moment in the orphanage when I got weepy and that's when we went down the hallway to the spot where my dad first said he wanted to adopt me. The memories of that moment flooded back fast and furious.

It was after the family who said they wanted to adopt me backed out. The story goes, after 10 years of trying, the couple found out they were going to have their own biological kid. And so even though they TOLD me they would be my new family and I spent a weekend at their house on a TEST-DRIVE, and slept in my new room that they had decorated just for me, they backed out of the deal.

I have my suspicions about the pregnancy thing. There's a chance that after being with them for 48 hours they were yet another person who decided I wasn't good enough to keep.

My dad found me crying in the corner of the hallway later that day, sucking my thumb (even though I was 4 and stopped years earlier) and wearing some lame orange jumper that looked like a onesie.

"Willa, sweetheart," he said, coming over to the corner and taking me into his arms, and there must have been something in his eye because he removed his glasses so he could wipe the corners. "How would you like to become a part of MY family?"

Even at that age I knew it was a pity offer, but beggars can't be choosers, so I said yes. And then, because I'd been crying so hard, I threw up Spaghetti-Os all over the front of his lab coat. He didn't seem to mind. He just took off his coat and then he pulled me to him in another hug, and he called me his "little girl." That's just what he said, "You're my little girl."

Now you can see why I love my dad, even though I know it's not cool to admit it. I know he had to work hard to convince Diane to agree to the adoption. Especially since her exact words were, "I need another kid like I need a hole in my head," when he suggested it. (And that's before she even MET me, so you know he had to jump through some major hoops to finally seal the deal.)

I think I might cry now, so I'm signing off. Children's Home insists they'll keep my address on file in case you come looking for me.

Willa

MAY 3, 4:07 P.M.

Dear M,

Next Sunday is Mother's Day and so my dad is taking Olivia and me shopping today to get something for Diane. Ugh! What do you get the person who has everything ... except compassion, love, patience, and common sense? If they sold those items at Macy's maybe I could pick up a case of each for Diane.

I'm kidding! Seriously, Diane is not as bad as I make her sound. It's all relative I suppose. Sure, compared to Mother Theresa or any TV mom, Diane is sorely lacking, but she's way better, let's say, than Mama Fratelli in the 1985 movie "The Goonies," or Cinderalla's stepmom, Lady Tremaine, so I take half of it back. Not half of the words, but like 50% off the top of each category.

In the past, Mother's Day has always made me

sad, but now that I have this diary I'm less sad about it. I'm trying to be optimistic that someday you'll read this and know a little more about me.

I think so far I've given you a pretty good background. Would you agree? Is there anything you'd like to know that I haven't addressed yet?

That's dumb, asking you questions. This isn't a pen pal deal where we send letters back and forth, so I don't know why I'm asking questions.

Back to Mother's Day ...

It's always been hard for me to give Diane a Mother's Day card because A. They are all too sappy for words, and B. None of them apply to her.

Most of them say stuff like "For everything you've done for me ..." "You are so special." "A true gift from above." ... blah blah blah.

So usually I have to buy her a generic one. You know the kind? The ones you'd give to your mail lady or your pet groomer, the lady who doesn't have any real kids, but instead has about 10 cats she pretends are her kids. The non-mushy cards that say something along the lines of "On Mother's Day" on the front, and then just has filler words about enjoying the day printed on the inside.

life sing peace wish hope

Sometimes it's hard to deal with the emotional drama of Mother's Day because Diane cries after opening her cards and presents from Olivia and my dad. Especially since Olivia does a number pouring on the baloney with her added sentiments handwritten inside the card.

And I should know how much baloney the words are because I'm the one who writes them for her. (Olivia finds it hard to string more than three words together in a sentence, so she pays me 50 cents a word to write them.)

If you want to know a secret, I sometimes pretend I'm Olivia when I write them, so the words mean something when I say "Thank you for the bedtime stories when I was little, and the butterfly kisses to wipe my tears. Thank you for believing in me when I didn't believe in myself, but most of all, thank you for your unconditional love."

Olivia doesn't even bother rewriting the words in her own writing, so it's been my words and my writing inside all of Diane's cards since I was 5 when I came to live with them. How funny that Diane has no idea what her daughter's writing looks like! And I don't mean that in a ha ha funny way, but in a "how bizarre" way. If I had a daughter, I'd like to think I'd be able to recognize her writing.

At least I'm in good company when it comes to the card thing because my dad's not big on the lovey dovey ones either. He usually gets Diane a funny one, those colorful cartoon kind with rabbits as the husband and wife and they're sitting on a sofa watching TV. I don't know why it's always rabbits. Why couldn't they use something else, like two lizards, or a couple of gazelles?

If I had to get you a present, I have no idea what I'd get you. Probably, I'd have to make you something because my allowance is ridiculous. Seriously, it's like one-tenth minimum wage. Olivia gets more of an allowance than I do and she literally has to do NOTHING. I kid you not, just the fact Olivia wakes up every morning makes her eligible, when instead I have a list of a million things I need to do to earn a pittance.

This is what I have to do:

I have to make my bed and clean my room. (Which is not that big of a deal to me, because I like having a clean room.)

I have to empty the dishwasher every day.

I have to empty all the trash cans in the bathrooms. (My dad takes out the trash in the kitchen.)

I have to set the table, and then clear the dishes after.

And I have to dry the pots and the pans. (My dad washes them.)

When I asked my dad why Princess Olivia doesn't have chores, my dad said it wasn't worth the hassle and that I could stop doing my chores anytime I wanted as long as I didn't mind living in a pig's sty. (My dad is devious that way. He knows there's no way I'd be able to survive living in a messy house!)

If I made you a present, I think it would be a calendar and I would fill it with doodles like I've done in the pages of this diary. Only I'd make sure they looked better than what you see here and I'd make the doodles appropriate to the theme of each month. If I knew your birthday month I would make that page really special. It would also be super helpful to know your name, because then I could incorporate it into the header of the page along with the flowers that represent your birth month.

That's it for now. Olivia is yelling at me she NEEDS me, which means I have to put on my thinking cap and come up with some words to write inside her mom's card.

In the meantime, here's a little something I wrote for you for Mother's Day.

Even though we are apart,

I carry you within my heart,

A special bond, like no other,

Is what I feel for you, my mother.

And even though you went away,

I think of you most every day.

HAPPY MOTHER'S DAY!

Love, Willa

MAY 13, 3:59 P.M.

Dear M,

I had the best day EVER!! I am NOT kidding; it may have been the very best. Or at least in the top 3.

This is what made it so terrific — My Social Studies class gave me a going-away party!!

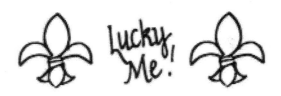

The party was spearheaded by Akshay and Georgie. They planned it to coincide with Georgie's 16th birthday, because Georgie knew his mom had already planned to bring a cake and balloons and stuff to celebrate his big day, and that meant they didn't need to do much. But the fact she also brought a SECOND cake, besides his chocolate birthday cake, a vanilla one made especially for me, and that it said "Good luck Willa" in green icing, well, it was all pretty spectacular in my book!

The class even pitched in and bought me some pink plastic sunglasses and some 100 SPF sunscreen, and they were wrapped in colored tissue paper. Instead of being inside a box the gifts were packaged inside an orange plastic sand bucket that came with a small green plastic shovel. (The things still had price tags on them and each only cost 99 cents, including the sand bucket, so everyone only had to give a dime which is pretty cheap if you think about it. But it's the thought that counts, right?)

After we had cake, Mrs. Hammersmith made everyone get up and say something nice about me. Most of the kids didn't even know who I am even though we've all attended school together for over 7 years.

Georgie went first and it was super embarrassing, because he told everyone he was going to miss his "girlfriend", which got quite a laugh. I am a girl and I am his friend, but I don't think of him in "that way," (and it has little to do with his having Downs and more to do with him being 16 and needing to shave.)

Then, since no one else volunteered, Akshay went next. He stood up and said how nice I was to him when he was new to school, and how I helped him escape from inside his locker on his first day. This also got quite a laugh from the class and even Mrs. Hammersmith laughed. I think she thought Akshay was joking, but, as we know, he wasn't.

Most of the kids just mumbled fake words when Mrs. Hammersmith made them stand to say something about me which came out sounding like "uh-hm mmm huh." A few kids said real words and some even said whole sentences! Zeke, he sits next to me on my right, said, "She seems smart," which I can only guess is because he's been copying off my paper the whole year, and so now he'll get an A in the class like me.

Desiree Turner, she sits in the second chair of the first row, said, "She turns her homework in on time," which proves she totally has noticed my existence and maybe was too shy or something to do anything about it.

Two boys, David Baxter and Peter Gold, said

they liked my backpack, (it's North Face) and one girl, Ellen, said I had SHINY HAIR. Shiny hair! When she said it, I almost started to cry. That is the NICEST compliment I've ever received in my WHOLE life! Shiny hair. I love it!!

Do you get the significance of the day, M?

H-SAM is about memory recall. And now, FINALLY, I have a super wonderful memory to relive! Anytime I'm sad, or lonely, all I have to do is call the memory to forefront of my consciousness and I'll relive it exactly as it was today! How cool is that?!

Another great thing that happened is we got our yearbooks this morning and where usually I only have five or six people who agree to sign my yearbook, (and most of them are teachers) Mrs. Hammersmith made EVERYONE in class sign my book! (There's a chance she offered them extra credit if they signed, but I don't know that for a fact.)

Akshay and Mrs. Hammersmith both added a few extra lines besides just signing their names, but they were the only ones and that includes Georgie, who's a big hugger, but not much with the written word. Still, it's so nice to see writing on the inside of my yearbook for a change. I only wish my other teachers would have made it a mandatory class assignment to sign my book. Except for Mrs. Hammersmith's class, none of the kids in my other classes would sign my book when I asked.

I am sooooooo happy!

Willa

MAY 14, 9:19 P.M.

Dear M,

I can't believe today is the last day I'll ever write to you from my bedroom in Chicago. Tomorrow is moving day, and as my dad says, "We are ready to rock and roll!"

The Pod is on its way to Cali, and Diane and Olivia are already in our new house. They took a plane out of O'Hare Airport the day after Mother's Day. Apparently, Olivia needed to be there on Tuesday so she could try out for the cheerleading squad at her new school, Huntington High. Or is it Huntington Harbor? Or maybe it's Huntington Harbor High. (That's H-SAM for ya. If it's not about me, I have a hard time remembering details.)

There's no furniture left in our house, so my dad and I have been sort of camping out, or as he calls it, "roughing it," only inside the house, not outside in nature. We've been sleeping in sleeping bags on the floor and cooking our meals on a portable camping stove. Even now I'm writing to you by the light of a Coleman lantern.

My dad messed up and gave the wrong cancellation date to the utility companies and they turned off the gas and electricity thinking we'd be gone. Luckily my dad forgot to call the water company or we wouldn't be able to use the toilets or shower, and there's NO WAY I'm peeing behind the hedges or washing myself with the hose as my dad suggested, so I could have a "true camping experience."

I have to say, M, I'm sad about leaving Chicago. And not just because I'm leaving Akshay and Georgie, who are even closer friends than I originally thought, or sad because I have to start all over in a new school without a single friend.

I'm sad because I really thought someday I'd see you walking down the street, a woman I didn't necessarily recognize, but someone I immediately KNEW. Or maybe the front doorbell would ring and I'd find you standing on the front steps of my house, a woman who looks much like me, only older, and apologizing it took so long to find me.

I don't know if I'll ever give up my dreams of having you find me, but one thing I know for sure; my dad was right. Having this diary really has given me perspective. Rereading the words on the pages has made me realize maybe I'm not such a loser.

Okay, maybe that's taking things a little too far. CLEARLY, a girl who once collected her fingernail clippings as a kid and kept them in a porcelain bowl on her nightstand IS a loser!

(But that was SO 5 years ago and I was going through a really difficult period in my life.)

Okay, I admit it; it wasn't fingernail, it was toe, but seriously, life was pretty unbearable at the time.

I also have come to realize maybe Diane and Olivia aren't as terrible as I make them out to be.

Naw... Scratch that. They both are pretty rotten. This isn't some fairytale where I wrap everything up in a shiny bow and we all live happily ever after.

But what I HAVE realized is everyone has a reason for why they act the way they do. Abusive parents were often abused as children, and I'm certainly not saying Diane is abusive, just that she's distant and unloving (to everyone but Olivia, who she's all over like a bad rash with all that Smother Love she gives her).

I try not to take Diane's poor treatment of me personally, because she's not even that nice to my dad. Between you and me, M, I have the feeling she's not all that "into him." I think she only married him because she couldn't find a real doctor to marry and so her only other choices were to marry a dentist or chiropractor, men who could still use the title DOCTOR after their names without going to a real medical school.

My point about Diane is that I believe she's cold and distant because her mom was that way with her. I've met her mom and believe me she's a ringer for Ursula the evil sea witch in "The Little Mermaid." Seriously, the resemblance is pretty stunning, even down to the blue eyeshadow and the red lipstick and the mole by the side of their lips.

I also have a theory why Olivia is such a cretin. I think underneath all Olivia's makeup and her beauty (AND her push-up bra) Olivia is super insecure. I have no idea why, but I know she is. And so that makes her a major show-off, always having to convince everyone she's ALL THAT because she worries she's not.

And lastly, I now know I have to accept some responsibility for my life. That if I want to HAVE friends, I need to BE a friend.

A girl I believed only looked THROUGH ME and never AT me, noticed I had shiny hair, and so what I originally thought — that I'm INVISIBLE, isn't true.

With just a little effort on my part, someday maybe more kids will begin to notice me ... remember I was in their classes at school for the past 7 years ... and sat next to them in science or played dodge ball with them in P.E.

Maybe if I put myself out there more they might notice that yes, I wear glasses, but behind my glasses are warm brown eyes the color of chocolate. Or that yes, I have a scar that runs from my lip to my nose, but when I smile they'll marvel at my perfect white teeth.

Or maybe, just maybe, someday, it won't be one SINGLE thing kids notice, but instead, they'll see all the parts of me together in one form, see me as a whole person, and they'll say, "There's that girl, Willa, she's someone I'd like to know."

Yours eternally,

Willa

 IT'S A PAWTY

Special thanks to the amazing folks at Kevin & Amanda Fonts for Peas for allowing the use of their amazing doodles. To download the FREE doodles used in this book, go to www.kevinandamanda.com

The following fonts were used:

Pea Karen's Doodles

Pea Fruit Salad Doodles

Pea Bethany's Doodles

Pea Cookie's Doodles

Pea Deliah's Doodles

Pea Deva McQueen

Pea Family Joy Doodles

Pea Jiawei Doodles

Pea Jillybean's Doodles

Pea Lauren Doodles

Pea Panda's Doodles

Pea Kiki Doodles

Pea KT Doodles

Pea Stacy's Doodles

Pea Stacy's New Doodles

Pea Shelly Belley's Doodles

Pea Tisha's Doodles

Pea KT Puppy Love Doodles

ABOUT THE AUTHOR

Linda Rey lives in Orange County, CA with her husband and a dog named Dude. Her favorite color is green, but blue is a close second. She'd rather eat potato chips than ice cream, but give her a donut and she'll be your friend for life. Linda's favorite books as a child were *The Secret Garden*, *Charlotte's Web*, and anything by Judy Blume. To get cool FREE stuff and her latest Nerdy Girl Books, go to www.NerdyGirlBooks.com or sign up for her newsletter at www.subscribepage.com/nerdywordz

A FAVOR – PRETTY PLEASE...

Do you enjoy reading and writing as much as I do? Would you like to see your words in print for all the world to see? Then here's your chance. All you have to do is write and post a quick REVIEW of Confessions of a Nerdy Girl: TOP SECRET to Amazon, Goodreads, or the retail source of this book. Whether short and sweet, or long and lyrical, I'd love to hear your thoughts.

Thanks so much!

XOXOXO

LINDA

COMING SOON!

Unlucky
Thirteen
Diary #2

Truth or Dare
Diary #3

Nerdy Ever
After A Nerdy
Novel: Book 1

WANT THE NEXT BOOK IN WILLA'S DIARY SERIES FOR FREE?

Go to http://www.subscribepage.com/nerdywordz to sign up, and not only will you get NERDY WORDZ, a 12-page word game, I'll also put you on a special list to get my newsletter, NERDY NEWS, where you'll have access to download Willa's next diary for FREE!

Go to www.NerdyGirlBooks.com for more info.

SAMPLE CHAPTER:

Confessions of a Nerdy Girl: Nerdy Ever
After
A NERDY NOVEL: BOOK 1

CHAPTER 1

"Hey, twerp." Blaine flicked her blonde ponytail and then shook a blue and white pom-pom in my face.

Following her lead, my adoptive sister, Olivia, copied her friend, ponytail toss and all. "Yeah, what's up, dork?"

I rolled my eyes at them and stepped aside to let them pass me in the hallway.

According to my lab experiment in Mr.

Bennett's science class, between the two of them there wasn't enough brainpower to illuminate a single light bulb. Not a standard one, either. I'm talking 4-watt night-light.

And what was up with the twerp and the dork?

"Watching those *Mean Girls* reruns again, have you, ladies?" I joked, pushing my glasses tighter against my nose and raising my eyebrows.

"Who you calling *ladies*?" Olivia snapped. "And it was *Pretty Little Liars*, not *Mean Girls*, weirdo. *Mean Girls* is so a hundred years ago."

"Actually, the movie premiered April 30, 2004. You're off by over a decade."

"See what I mean?" Olivia looked at Blaine and shook her head in disgust. "Could she be any weirder? I can't believe my parents adopted her. Honestly, Blaine, you have no idea what it's like to live with an artistic savant."

I rolled my eyes skyward before settling them on Olivia's perfect face. "First, the word you're looking for is *autistic*, not artistic, and second, 'savant' is pronounced like want, and not like ant or pant."

"Who *cares*?" She roughly brushed my shoulder, and the two crossed the threshold into Olivia's den of darkness, slamming the door behind them.

"Is she really autistic?" I heard Blaine say. "She looks normal-ish."

I didn't hear Olivia's answer because by then I was halfway down the hallway.

Despite what Olivia said, I'm not an autistic savant, which the dictionary defines as a person affected with a mental disability who shows exceptional skills in mathematics or music. As a matter of fact, I pretty much suck at both math and music. Unless, of course, we're referring to my ability to *listen* to music. In which case I do okay.

But it's not as though I'm normal, either.

Medical books list me as "MS." It's short for "Minor Shisbey," and I'm number thirteen. Make that *unlucky* thirteen. I'm the thirteenth documented person in the world to have something called H-SAM, Highly Superior Auto Biographical Memory. I'm also the last documented case, unless someone else has come out of the H-SAM closet that I don't know about.

Having H-SAM doesn't make me a genius or anything, and it doesn't give me a photographic memory. It just means I can recall any information personally linked to me. The things I saw or heard. How things smelled, or the way I felt.

Not that there's anything super fantastic to tell so far. At thirteen, I think I'm stuck in a commercial break and all the good stuff must happen in the second half of the show.

I can recall, with complete accuracy, all the memories of my life, stored in my brain like information on a computer hard drive and with the ability to retrieve them in an instant whether I want to or not. Not my actual birth, of course, that would be a stretch, not to mention gross, but beginning the day after my first birthday when my birth mom held me in her arms and knocked on the door of the Children's Home Society of Chicago, crying to the woman who answered that she just couldn't keep me anymore.

You probably think I'm famous for being number thirteen, but I'm not. At least not in the real world. You won't see me on talk shows like *Good Morning* … (insert city here), or *Good Day* … (same thing). Unless you're one of the doctors at the Department of Neurology at the University of California, who tested me and knew my real name—correction, my *adopted* name,

because I don't know my real last name—
I'll go down in history as just MS.

My full name is Wilhelmina Eugenia
Shisbey, (I know, right? Could it be any
worse?) but people call me Willa. My
records are sealed, so I don't know much
about my birth parents, but I'm told my
mother named me after Wilhelmina
Cooper, the famous model who started one
of the top modeling agencies in New York
City back in the 60s. Maybe it's a lie, or
maybe it's not.

I'd like to think it's the truth. That
sometime before I was born, before my
mother saw her hopes dashed the minute
she saw me—a homely kid with a cleft lip
and a wonky eye—that she had big dreams
for me. I still don't know where the Eugenia

came from, but I do know I'd love to send it back from wherever it was. (Like 258 AD, the last time the name was popular.) Shisbey I inherited four years later, when my adoption became final after my dad, Ted Shisbey, who had been my dentist at the orphanage, and his wife, Diane, took me into their home.

A home that unfortunately also included their eight-year-old biological daughter, Olivia. To say Olivia has hated me from the start would not be an exaggeration and eight years later things are definitely NOT improving.

The door to Olivia's room swung open and Olivia stuck her head out. In the reflection of the mirrored closet doors I saw Blaine practicing cheer moves between selfie shots.

"Oh, I forgot to tell you," Olivia blew a bubble with her gum and let it pop before finishing, "your little friend is outside. She wanted to know if you could come out and *play*."

Both Dumb and Dumber thought the line was pure gold and collapsed into a fit of giggles.

Marley Applegate is my new best friend and she has a dry sense of humor most people don't get. (Her "come out and play" line was a joke, Olivia. Duh!) I met Marley the first day I attended school in California after moving from Lincoln Park, a suburb in Chicago. It was May 16th, a Thursday, and just three weeks before the end of the school year.

Diane and Olivia had already been here for a couple of weeks so Olivia could qualify for the cheer team at Huntington Harbor. Dad and I stayed behind while he tied up the loose ends with his dental practice and worked out the details of his new partnership. I had two weeks without Olivia … or her mom, (who I will never consider *my* mom). It was just Dad and me. Pure bliss.

The day I met Marley she came up to me at the Friendship Bench where I sat, alone, eating my lunch. In case you haven't heard of it, the Friendship Bench is the place where all the nerds go to find another nerd to befriend. Once successfully paired, you're required to pay it forward and return to the bench to introduce yourself to the next student too shy or uncool to meet people without the aid of a hookup point. The hope is eventually all the nerds and the misfits in the school will have met.

Think of the Friendship Bench as the Match.com of the geeks and the socially awkward.

Marley is half-black, small for her age, and super smart. She has some crazy-high IQ and is the editor of the school paper. Marley is the only person I know who hates her name almost as much as I hate mine. But if you ask me, it's not even close. Marley May Applegate versus Wilhelmina Eugenia Shisbey. *No way, Jose.* Sorry, Mar, I win this, hands down.

"I'm going to the beach!" I yelled out to my dad, hearing the chop chop of his kitchen knife hitting the butcher block as he sliced carrots. My dad's sort of a nerd like me, and he has a garden in the backyard. Most California kids get a pool. I get an organic vegetable garden and smelly compost pile.

"Don't forget your sunscreen! And have fun!"

I let the front-door screen slam behind me and joined Marley seated on my front steps, her eyes closed and her face turned up to catch the sun. She was dressed in orange shorts, a geometric patterned T-shirt, and green flip-flops with plastic daisies glued on. Collectively, her outfit represented every color of the sherbets in the front counter at Baskin Robbins ice cream.

Because she's small for twelve, (Marley skipped a grade) her wardrobe choices are limited to the kids' section, which means Marley has a closet full of pastels and patterns and the occasional cartoon graphic tee—a look only she can pull off. Marley also wears pigtails she calls dreadlocks, but I say are curls she just doesn't brush.

As far as I'm concerned, in all of nerdom at Triton Middle School, Marley reigns supreme. She could not care less what people think about her wardrobe choices. Unlike me, who can obsess over minutia, (darn OCD!) and is the reason I stick to a uniform that consists of a white long-sleeved button-down shirt, denim jeans, and black-and-white Converse sneakers whatever the season.

"Hey, Marley." I sat down beside her and gave her a little nudge. "Working on your tan?" I joked.

Marley's skin is the color of the outside of a Kit Kat bar, so it's not as if she needs to tan. Lucky duck. Not me, my skin is the same color as the inside of a Peppermint Pattie, white as snow. I burn to a crisp no matter how much sunscreen I glob on. Even this early into the game, I don't think sunny California is going to be a good match for me.

Marley nudged me back. "Hey yourself, four-eyes. Ready to go?" Marley didn't wait for me to answer and she stood up, dusting off her backside. She took her arm in mine and we started walking down the street toward the beach a few blocks away.

Marley's four-eyes remark is an inside joke. There's not an unkind bone in Marley's body. Yes, I wear glasses—thick black-framed ones to help with my astigmatism and to keep my weak eye from ever turning back in. But that's not why Marley said it. The reason Marley calls me four-eyes is she insists I have eyes in the back of my head. Some sort of sixth sense, she tells me.

In a way, Marley's right. For some reason I can feel what people are feeling. Even if they are yards away from me, I can *feel* them. Their joy or their sorrow, or if they're angry or anxious. It's called empathy and it's probably from my years in the orphanage. And I don't want to get all

Lemony Snicket on you about my days in the orphanage, because they weren't all terrible—if you don't count having to take baths with other kids or sleeping three to a bed, but it was hard not to suck up what the other kids were feeling. The sadness and the despair. The desperate desire to become part of a family.

Marley and I didn't make it four houses down the block before I gently untangled my arm from hers. As the new kid in town, I didn't want any of the other kids on our block to get the wrong idea about me. Or Marley. Not that there would be anything wrong if Marley liked girls in *that* way. To each his or her own, as far as I'm concerned. But Marley definitely wasn't gay or anything. She was affectionate to everyone—boys and girls—

and so sometimes kids got the wrong idea about her.

Marley has suffered through more than her share of vicious rumors. Not only because of being named after a major Rasta stoner, but also because of the biracial thing, and the fact she's the editor of the school paper. Just last week, some brain-dead goofball wrote in red lipstick on Marley's locker, *Militant Marley for Congress*.

As if anyone who dresses like Rainbow Brite could be a radical. I'm so sure.

"Don't frown, Willa. It will give you wrinkles." Marley smiled at me. "You think too much. You need to learn to be more in the moment," she said, sounding like some New Age guru. Marley palmed the button on the light pole and we waited for it to say *walk*.

"*Omm ...*" I chanted, closing my eyes and touching my thumbs to my index fingers in what I imagined was a close representation of the standard yoga finger position.

The light changed, and we crossed the busy intersection and turned right at the sidewalk heading towards the lifeguard station to meet up with members of our school's surf club for beach clean-up day. It was purely voluntary, but unlike Marley, who believes "it's our civic duty to protect Mother Earth who sustains us," I was only in it for the extra credit in my fourth period class.

Despite the closeness of the water and

not yet 10:00 in the morning, I was starting to sweat. Maybe I needed to go to a tanning salon and build up a fake tan first, so I could wear a short-sleeved shirt like a normal person. Although most normal people don't have as much disgusting dark hair on their white arms as I have. Maybe a tan would at least lessen the contrast. I'd still have hairy arms, but on darker skin, (and the melanoma won't show up for another ten years, if I'm lucky).

My hair was making my neck sweat, so I pulled two rubber bands from my wrists and put my hair into pigtails before unbuttoning my shirt one button.

One button or five, it wouldn't have mattered, there's not much to see.

"So, who do you think will show up?" I

asked, but especially caring about one *who* in particular.

Marley's face split in a big grin. "The way you're blushing, I know who you hope will be there." Marley fished a pair of neon green sunglasses out of her pocket and put them on. She scanned the beach and then pointed. "There's your guy right there. He's under the Surfrider tent."

My guy, Marley called him. *In my dreams* ...

Cody Cassidy, the coolest of the cool, stood under the blue pop-up tent along with a half dozen other people, both kids and adults. He was leaning over the portable table instructing some blonde-haired girl where to sign in. She smiled at him—how could she *not?*—and Cody handed her some gloves and a trash bag from the pile on top of the table.

The event was co-sponsored by Hurley, so Cody was completely Hurleyed out, and he wore black Hurley board shorts with green neon stitching and drawstring, a classic Hurley T-shirt in green with black block lettering, and a black Sig Zane trucker hat covering his dark blond hair. I couldn't be sure from the distance, but it looked like he was wearing black flip-flops. Hurley Phantoms, maybe.

Six months ago, I wouldn't have known the difference between Hurley and girly, but then six months ago I wasn't living in Huntington Beach, just blocks away from the hottest boy I'd ever seen. And if I know anything at all about boys, (which I don't, so I had to break down and f

Olivia), it's that in order to inter

you have to find some common ground. Olivia suggested I show an interest in whatever the boy liked. That's why I now have a current subscription to *Surfer Magazine.* I don't know shoot from shinola about girls' clothes, but I'm becoming a walking Wikipedia of the current trends in boy's surfing apparel.

I met Cody the first day at Triton. Not at the Friendship Bench, of course. Kids like him don't have to go looking for friends. Popular kids like Cody are the sun, the center of the solar system, and everyone else just revolves around them.

I met Cody in second period, at exactly 9:28 a.m., right after Mr. Spitzer finished taking roll. Mr. Spitzer mortified me beyond belief when he called the "newbie" up to the front of the room. He actually called me that—the *newbie*. As in, "Let's all meet the newbie, Wilhelmina Shisbey," which of course brought on coughs and giggles, because, come on, who else but me can lay claim to an old-fashioned name like Wilhelmina? Certainly no one in Orange County, California, where all the kids have these made-up sounding names their parent's got from watching those Disney Channel teen shows.

Here's just a small sampling of the names: There are the twins, Dakota and Dallas, and their brother, Denver, who is Olivia's new boyfriend. According to Olivia, the Duncan kids are named after the places where they were conceived. But, hello!—there's a *North* and a *South* Dakota, and it's over a thousand miles from Rapid City, South Dakota, to Dallas, Texas. I may not know much about s-e-x, but I'm willing to bet my allowance you can't conceive twins in two different places that are a thousand miles apart.

Some of the other random names of my new California classmates are: Braden, Brylee, Hallie, Keiran, Griffen, Kirby, and Jax. Not Jack, but *Jax*. J-A-X. And not to change the subject, but how is it possible almost all the kids at Triton Middle School have hair that is white-blonde, blonde-blonde, golden blonde, or blond*ish*? I mean, is it even statistically possible? Isn't it even *less* probable than two blue-eyed parents having a brown-eyed kid? You know, that broken gene, dominant trait thing?

Anyway … back to the story of how I met Cody.

I didn't immediately leap from my seat that day when Mr. Spitzer called me up, so he turned up the wick and he did this theatrical sweeping motion with his hands, and he bowed at the waist, inviting me up. On my way to the board, one of the Duncan twins intentionally pushed her backpack to the floor and I stumbled over it. Everybody laughed again—at the nerdy new kid tripping her way up the aisle. Cody, nice guy that he is, reached out a hand to steady me, which made it worse.

I couldn't tell if it was the girl with the city

name or the one with the abbreviated state, but one of them said, "Eww, Cody," as if we were still in third grade and she thought maybe I had cooties or something.

Once I got to the front, I stuttered through my introduction, my heart hammering in my chest, before I finally managed to say, "My name is Wilhelmina, but people call me Willa."

"She looks more like Ugly Betty than Wilhelmina Slater," someone muttered, commenting on the *Ugly Betty* TV show, and not the first time I'd heard the line before.

"Yeah, right?" someone else said.

"True dat!" And it may have been the single black kid, Trey, in Wonder-Bread-white-land who said it, but I don't want to profile.

I took a deep breath and continued, looking out into the sea of faces and trying to picture the kids in their underwear like my dad once suggested in order to make public speaking easier, but it seemed wrong on *sooo* many levels, so I quit trying, and instead I stared down at the tops of my shoes. "I just moved here with my family from Lincoln Park. That's in Illinois, about four miles from the city of Chicago."

From the back of the room, a voice called out in falsetto, "I like to take long walks on the beach at sunset and my fondest dream is to someday marry Nick Jonas."

Mr. Spitzer stopped shuffling the papers

on his desk and glared at someone in the last row. "That's enough, Dylan."

Dylan slunk down in his seat, but gave a down-low high-five to the kid seated across the row from him.

"Thank you, Willa, you may sit down." Mr. Spitzer adjusted his gold wire-rimmed glasses and said the line I guess he's paid to say: "On behalf of the faculty, I'd like to formally welcome you to Triton Middle School. Class, let's all use some of our Dolphin spirit and welcome Willa."

A few kids said hi or hey and smiled, but most stayed silent, and a few stared me down, or maybe they sized me *up*. Whatever it was, it seemed slightly threatening.

One voice, however, rang out loud and clear. It was Cody's. "Welcome to sunny California, Chicago," he said, a genuine smile on his handsome face, and renaming me after the windy city. "You're gonna love it here."

To get notified when *Nerdy Ever After* is available, sign up for Nerdy News at: www.NerdyGirlBooks.com

Made in the USA
Columbia, SC
22 April 2020